Renewals can be made
by internet   www.onfife.com/fife-libraries
in person   at any library in Fife
by phone   03451 55 00 66

AT FIFE
LIBRARIES

Thank you for using your library

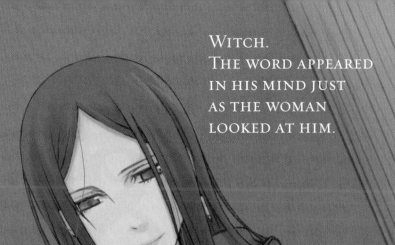

WITCH.
THE WORD APPEARED
IN HIS MIND JUST
AS THE WOMAN
LOOKED AT HIM.

"YOU'RE QUITE A HANDSOME MAN.
BUT YOU THINK ME A WITCH—
I CAN SEE IT IN YOUR EYES."

"IN THAT CASE, PERHAPS
THAT'S HOW I SHOULD
INTRODUCE YOU?"

—DIANA RUBENS,
THE CHRONICLER

—Gi Batos,
the Merchant

RIGHT THEN AND THERE, AMATI HELD UP A DAGGER AND A SHEET OF PARCHMENT AND MADE HIS DECLARATION.

"I WILL PAY THE DEBT THAT NOW WEIGHS UPON THE SLENDER SHOULDERS OF THIS TRAVELING NUN—AND WHEN THIS GODDESS OF LOVELINESS DOES REGAIN HER FREEDOM, I SWEAR BY SAINT LAMBARDOS, WHO WATCHES OVER THIS ROWEN TRADE GUILD, THAT HOLO THE NUN WILL HAVE MY UNDYING LOVE!"

—AMATI,
THE FISHMONGER

THEY WERE
NOT WORDS
THAT COULD
BE SAID
LIGHTLY.

"YOU HAVE
ME, DON'T
YOU?"
HE SAID,
COMPLETELY
SERIOUS.

BUT HOLO
MERELY
SCOFFED
AND SHOT
BACK, "WHAT
ARE YOU TO
ME? NAY—
WHAT AM
I TO YOU?"

Contents

VOLUME III

ISUNA HASEKURA

Yen
Press

NEW YORK

SPICE AND WOLF, Volume 3
ISUNA HASEKURA

Translation: Paul Starr

OOKAMI TO KOUSHINRYO © Isuna Hasekura /
ASCII MEDIA WORKS Inc. 2006. All rights reserved.
First published in Japan in 2006 by MEDIA WORKS
INC., Tokyo. English translation rights in USA, Canada, and
UK arranged with ASCII MEDIA WORKS INC. through
Tuttle-Mori Agency, Inc., Tokyo.

English translation © 2010 by Hachette Book Group, Inc.

Yen Press
Hachette Book Group
237 Park Avenue, New York, NY 10017

www.HachetteBookGroup.com
www.YenPress.com

Yen Press is an imprint of Hachette Book Group, Inc.
The Yen Press name and logo are trademarks of Hachette
Book Group, Inc.

First Yen Press Edition: December 2010

Library of Congress Cataloging-in-Publication Data
Hasekura, Isuna, 1982–
  [Ookami to Koushinryo. English]
  Spice & Wolf. vol. III / Isuna Hasekura ; illustrated by
Jyuu Ayakura ; [translation by Paul Starr]. — 1st Yen Press ed.
    p. cm.
  Summary: Having narrowly escaped financial ruin,
Lawrence turns his attention to helping Holo find her
ancient homeland in the North, but when a rival merchant
sets his sights on the beautiful Wolf-God, Lawrence must
ask himself whether his relationship with her is business or
pleasure.
  ISBN 978-0-7595-3107-9
  [1. Fantasy. 2. Merchants—Fiction. 3. Goddesses—
Fiction. 4. Wolves—Fiction.] I. Ayakura, Jyuu, 1981– ill.
II. Starr, Paul Tuttle. III. Title. IV. Title: Spice and
Wolf.
PZ7.H2687Spm 2010
[Fic]—dc22   2010015689

10 9 8 7 6 5 4

BRR

Printed in the United States of America

SPICE & WOLF

CHAPTER ONE

Lawrence and Holo were six days out of Ruvinheigen. With each passing day, the cold grew more severe, and the sky remained frustratingly cloudy, so that even at the height of noonday, the meager wind was enough to bring a chill.

Once they drew alongside the river, the cold from the mist combined with the frigid air to make it that much more bitter.

Even the river water looked icy. It was hazy, as though the cloudy sky itself had melted into the flow.

However Lawrence and Holo may have been bundled up in secondhand winter-weather clothing they had bought in Ruvinheigen, cold was still cold.

Nevertheless, the frosty edge was dulled when Lawrence reflected with a mixture of chagrin and nostalgia on the times when, as a young merchant, he had to forego cold-weather gear in favor of cargo.

Evidently, seven years of experience would whip even a rank amateur like him into some kind of shape.

Besides the warm clothing, there was something else that mitigated the cold this year.

Lawrence had now entered the winter of his seventh year as a merchant since becoming independent at age eighteen, and he looked sideways at the person sitting next to him in the driver's seat.

Typically, he'd sat in that seat alone.

Even on those rare occasions when he did happen to be traveling with another, he would not sit in the driver's seat with Lawrence — and they certainly wouldn't have shared the same tarp over their knees for warmth.

"Is aught the matter?" asked his companion, her slightly archaic speech evident as ever.

She was a lovely girl who appeared to be in her teens, with a stunning fall of chestnut hair that would have been the envy of any noblewoman.

But what Lawrence envied was neither her flowing locks nor the expensive robe wrapped about her body.

No, what he envied was the thickly furred tail that lay across her lap as she carefully groomed it.

It was the same chestnut brown as her hair, save for its snow-white tip, and the tail was every inch as warm as it appeared to be. Were it made into a stole it would be every nobleman's wife's object of desire, but unfortunately, it was not for sale.

"Will you hurry your grooming and put your tail under the tarp again?"

Sitting there wrapped in a robe, neatly combing her tail fur, Holo looked for all the world like a nun doing some kind of handicraft.

She shot Lawrence an unpleasant glance with her red-tinged brown eyes before her lips parted, showing a flash of white fangs.

"My tail is not your personal muffler."

The tail in question flicked slightly.

That same tail, which a passing traveler or merchant would surely mistake for a simple fur of some kind, was indeed attached to its original owner, who so fastidiously groomed it. And she didn't just have a tail; underneath her hood was also a pair of pointed wolf ears.

Naturally, these ears and tail indicated that she was no mere human.

Though there were people who, possessed by fairies or demons, had this or that inhuman feature when they were born, this girl was not such a person.

Her true form was that of a colossal wolf who dwelled within wheat; she was Holo, the Wisewolf of Yoitsu. An adherent of the common Church faith would fear such an entity as a pagan god, but Lawrence was past such fear.

He was much more likely to reappropriate the tail Holo was so proud of as a lap warmer.

"It's such fine fur, though; putting it under the tarp keeps my legs as warm as a mountain of pelts would."

Just as Lawrence hoped, Holo sniffed proudly and tucked her tail back underneath the tarp across their legs.

"Anyway, will we make the town soon? We will arrive before the day is out, no?"

"Just a bit farther along this river," said Lawrence.

"And then, finally, a hot meal. I've had my fill of cold gruel. I can't stand another bite!"

Lawrence could brag of more experience eating bad cooking than Holo could, but he was in complete agreement with her.

Eating well was one of the few pleasures of travel, but even that pleasure disappeared with the arrival of winter.

In the freezing cold, the only choices were crusty rye bread or porridge made from the same, with tasteless jerky or those few vegetables that could be stored for long periods of time—garlic and onions.

With her keen sense of smell, Holo couldn't eat the aforementioned garlic or onions, and though she hated the bitter taste of rye bread, she managed to choke it down with water.

For Holo the glutton, this was not far from torture.

"Well, the town we're bound for is in the middle of a huge fair, so you can look forward to all kinds of food."

"Oh ho. But will your coin purse handle such extravagance?"

A week earlier in the city of Ruvinheigen, Lawrence's greed led him to fall into a desperate trading company's trap, and he had been on the verge of accepting complete ruin.

However, after a series of twists, he avoided that but still had not turned a profit, and indeed had come away with some loss.

As for the armor that was the cause of it all, he had wound up unloading it in Ruvinheigen for rock-bottom prices rather than transporting the heavy goods farther north, where prices were likely to be even worse.

Despite Holo's frequent requests to buy her this or that bauble, her last remark showed some consideration for Lawrence's rather dire straits.

She was frequently abrasive and high-handed, but her heart was fundamentally a good one.

"Don't worry, your food bill's within the budget."

Holo still seemed to be worried about something. "Mm…"

"Besides, I wound up not being able to get you those honeyed peach preserves I promised you. Just think of it as payment for that."

"'Tis true…and yet…"

"What?"

"I'm half-worried about your balance but half-worried about myself. If I eat too extravagantly, we'll have to stay in that much poorer lodgings."

Lawrence smiled in understanding. "Well, I was planning on

staying in a decent inn. Surely you're not going to tell me it must have separate bedrooms with a fireplace in each?"

"I would not go so far as that, but it won't do to have you use my appetite as an excuse."

"An excuse for what?"

Lawrence looked ahead to correct the horse's path, at which point Holo leaned over and whispered in his ear, "For only renting a single bed, saying you lack the coin to do more. Sometimes I prefer to sleep alone."

Lawrence yanked on the reins, and the horse neighed its uncertainty.

Having become quite used to this sort of teasing from Holo, he was quick to recover.

He forced calm to his face and gave her a cold look. "I'm not sure someone who snores so readily should be talking."

Perhaps taken aback by the rapidity of Lawrence's recovery, Holo drew away from him, twisting her lip unpleasantly.

Lawrence pressed the attack, so as not to let this rare opportunity for victory escape.

"Besides, you're hardly my type."

Holo's keen ears could easily tell truth from lies.

What Lawrence had just said was — just barely — not a lie.

Holo's face froze, perhaps from surprise at the truth of Lawrence's words.

"Surely you know I'm telling the truth," said Lawrence, closing in on the final blow.

Holo stared at him, dumbfounded for a moment, her mouth opening and closing wordlessly. Eventually she realized that her response itself was letting Lawrence get the better of her.

Her ears drooped underneath her hood, and she looked down, dejected.

It was Lawrence's first victory in quite some time.

Nonetheless, it was not a true victory.

While it was not precisely a lie to say that Holo wasn't Lawrence's type, neither was it precisely the truth.

All he needed to do was tell her as much, and his revenge for all the times he had suffered as her plaything would be complete.

He reflected on how fond he was of Holo's laughing face or how innocent she looked as she slept.

And, indeed, her dejected mien was quite dear to him, as well.

Or, put another way—

"So you like to see me this way, do you?"

Lawrence met Holo's upturned gaze and was unable to stop himself from blushing.

"Such foolishness. The more idiot the male, the weaker a girl he fancies, never realizing his head is the weakest part of all," mocked Holo, flashing her white fangs as she turned the tables on Lawrence.

"If I'm to be the helpless princess, you'll need to play the intrepid knight. And yet what are you, really?"

She pointed her finger at him and pressed him for an answer.

Countless scenes flashed through Lawrence's mind—scenes that served as a painful reminder that he was no chosen knight, but an ordinary traveling merchant.

Holo gave a short sigh, evidently satisfied by his reaction, but then she put her index finger to her chin as something seemed to occur to her.

"Though come to that, I suppose you are a knight of sorts. Hm."

Lawrence sifted through his memories but could not think of any time when he had been particularly gallant.

"What, have you forgotten? Did you not stand between me and my attackers? 'Twas in the tunnels beneath Pazzio, during that silver coin nonsense."

"...Oh, that."

Lawrence remembered the incident but still didn't feel particularly knightly. He had been shaking so badly he could barely stand, his clothes in tatters.

"It's not physical strength that makes a knight. 'Twas the first time I've been protected by anyone."

Holo smiled sheepishly and drew near to Lawrence. The rapidity of her mood swings was always alarming—fast enough to make a merchant, even one used to the vicissitudes of profit and loss, run away screaming.

Lawrence, however, had nowhere to run.

"And you'll look after me henceforth, yes?" The "wolf" smiled a soft, innocent smile that was distinctly kittenish. No hardworking merchant, used to years of toil and travel, had any right to see such a smile.

But the smile was fake. Holo was still angry at Lawrence's claim that she was not his type—extremely angry, in all likelihood.

Lawrence was well aware of this.

"...Sorry."

Like magic, Holo's smile became genuine when she heard that word. She sat up and giggled indulgently. "That's what I like about you."

In their back-and-forth teasing, Holo and Lawrence were like two frolicking pups.

In the end, they were very comfortable with each other.

"Anyhow, I suppose I don't mind a single bed, but I'll take twice as much dinner to compensate."

"I know, I know," answered Lawrence, wiping the unpleasant sweat from his brow—it wasn't even cold.

Holo raised her voice in a laugh once more. "So, what's tasty in this part of the world?"

"The local specialty, you mean? Well, I don't know if it counts as a specialty, really, but..."

"Fish, is it not?"

Lawrence was about to say just that, so Holo's quick answer surprised him.

"Indeed, it is. Yes, west of here there's a lake. Dishes made with fish taken from that lake are what passes for the local specialty. But how did you know?"

Holo could generally discern people's motives, but Lawrence didn't think she could simply read his mind like that.

"Oh, I've just been catching the scent on the wind," she said, pointing to the opposite shore of the river along which they traveled. "That caravan, it's carrying fish."

Lawrence looked and noticed for the first time a caravan of wagons that was so far away it was all he could manage to count them — he certainly couldn't tell what they carried. The caravan would probably meet up with Lawrence and Holo eventually, based on the direction and speed with which the horses were pulling the wagons.

"Though I can't fathom what a fish dish would be. Would it be anything like the eel we had in Ruvinheigen?"

"That was just fried in oil. There are more involved dishes — steamed with meat or vegetables or cooked with spices. Also, this town's got another specialty."

"Oh ho!" Holo's eyes glinted, and beneath the tarp, her tail wagged to and fro in anticipation.

"You can look forward to it once we get there."

Holo puffed her cheeks out a bit in frustration at Lawrence's teasing, but she was far from angry.

"What say you to buying some fish from yonder caravan if they prove to be of good quality?" she asked.

"I don't have an eye for fish. I took a loss on dealing fish once, so I try to avoid them."

"But you've my eyes and nose now."

"Can you sniff out the quality of fish?"

"I've half a mind to sniff out your quality!" said Holo with a mischievous smile. Lawrence had to surrender.

"Mercy, please! I suppose if they have anything worth buying, we can pick some up and have it prepared for us in town. It's a better deal that way, too."

"Quite! You may rely on me."

Though it wasn't exactly clear where Holo and Lawrence would meet up with the caravan that ostensibly carried fish, the distance between the two was steadily closing. Lawrence guided the horse down the road.

And yet—thought Lawrence to himself, looking first to the caravan, then aside at his traveling companion.

If her eyes and nose were good enough to tell the quality of a fish, perhaps she really could take the measure of a person the same way.

Lawrence laughed the notion off, but it still nagged at him.

He casually brought his right shoulder up to his nose and took a whiff. Despite living on the road, he didn't think he smelled too bad—and Holo herself had but a single change of clothes.

He was mulling this excuse over when he felt a gaze upon him.

"Goodness. You really are so charming, I've no idea what to do with myself," said Holo, exasperated.

Lawrence had no response.

The river flowed so slowly that at a glance, it seemed not to be moving at all. Soon, people who had stopped to let their horses drink or shift their loads came into view. There was also a rare traveling sword sharpener—a sword stuck in the ground served in place of a sign. The sword sharpener yawned, chin in hands, leaning on his large whetstone.

There was also a raft moored at a pier, where a knight stood with his horse, arguing with the boatman. The knight was only lightly equipped, so he was probably a messenger from this or that fort. Most likely, the boatman did not want to embark on a trip without more passengers, which was the source of the argument.

Lawrence himself had been angry at boatmen unwilling to set out when he was in a hurry, so the scene brought a pained smile to his face.

As the land shifted from endless wild plains to cultivated farmland, peasants doing their work popped up more and more frequently.

No matter how many times he saw it, a change of scenery that came along with human activity always made Lawrence happy.

It was about then that that Holo and Lawrence finally met up with the caravan.

There were three wagons in all, each drawn by a pair of horses. The wagons lacked drivers' seats, and one well-dressed man sat in the bed of the last cart while a hired laborer guided each cart as he walked.

Lawrence was impressed by the extravagance of using two horses per wagon, but as they got closer to the caravan, he realized it was not just for show.

Piled on the wagon beds were barrels and crates big enough to hold a person. Some had been filled with water — apparently for the captured fish to swim in.

Unsalted fish of any kind was a luxury. Live fish was all the more so.

Although the transport of live fish was rare in and of itself, there was something else about the caravan that surprised Lawrence even more.

The person who evidently transported these three large wagons of fresh fish was a merchant even younger than Lawrence.

"Fish, you say?" said the young man in the last cart, responding to Lawrence's question. He wore the traditional oiled leather coat of a fishmonger.

"Yes, I was wondering if you might sell me a few," said Lawrence, who had traded places with Holo.

The young merchant's reply was quick. "I'm terribly sorry, all of our fish have been spoken for already."

It was an unexpected answer; the young man seemed to realize the surprise he had caused in Lawrence, and he pulled back his hood to show his face properly.

The young man's face was as boyish as his youthful voice. Though he could not strictly be called a "boy," he was certainly not yet twenty. Fishmongers were a generally rough and manly lot, but this young man was unusually slender. His wavy blond hair only added to his aura of refinement.

Even if the man was as young as he looked, the fact that he transported three wagonloads of fresh fish meant he was not a merchant to be underestimated.

"You'll pardon me for asking, but are you a traveling merchant?" asked the lad.

Lawrence couldn't tell whether the young man's smile was genuine or mercantile, but in any case, the only reasonable response was to smile back. "Yes, I've just come from Ruvinheigen."

"I see. Well, there's a lake about a half day's journey up the road we've just come down. I'm sure you can deal with the fishermen there. They're bringing in excellent carp of late."

"Ah, no, I'm not buying for business. I was merely hoping you could sell me a few fish for dinner. That is all."

The young merchant's smile quickly disappeared in favor of surprise — this was probably the first time he had heard such a request.

A merchant hauling salted fish over long distances would be

quite used to selling a little on the road, but such a practice was quite out of the ordinary when transporting fresh fish from a nearby lake.

The young merchant's expression of surprise soon shifted to one of careful consideration.

Having met with an unexpected situation, he was probably trying to decide whether there was a new business to be had here.

"You're quite serious about your trade," said Lawrence.

"Oh —," said the lad, returning to himself and obviously flustered. "My apologies! Er, incidentally, if you're looking for fish for dinner, you must be stopping in Kumersun, yes?"

"Indeed. For the winter market and also to take in the festival."

Kumersun was the name of the city they were bound for, just in time for the town's great market, which was held twice a year in the summer and the winter.

There was also a festival that coincided with the winter market.

Lawrence didn't know the specifics, but he had heard it was a pagan celebration that would make any devout follower of the Church faint dead away.

Six days' travel north from Ruvinheigen, a city which even now functioned as a resupply depot for Church-funded incursions against pagans, relations between Church followers and pagans were not as simple as they were in the south.

The nation that controlled the vast lands north of Ruvinheigen was known as Ploania, and there were many pagans among the royalty and nobility there. It was only natural that there would be cities where the Church and pagans coexisted.

Kumersun belonging as it did to the nobility of Ploania, distanced itself from troublesome religious issues. It was a large town devoted to economic prosperity, and the Church was forbidden from proselytizing there. Inquiring as to whether the town's festival was of the Church faith or the pagan one was likewise prohibited — the explanation being that it was simply a tradition of the town.

Given that such festivals were a rarity and that pagans could safely attend them, people would pack themselves into the town every year to attend the event, which was known as the Laddora festival.

Based on what Lawrence had heard, he planned to arrive a bit early in order to beat the crowds, but it seemed he'd been naive.

"Might I ask if you've already arranged for accommodations?" asked the young merchant with worry on his face.

"The festival is the day after tomorrow. Surely the inns aren't all occupied already."

"I assure you, they are."

Holo shifted restlessly next to Lawrence, no doubt worried about where they would stay.

Whatever her abilities in wolf form, Holo's human form was just as susceptible to cold as a true human. She wanted to get out of the cold weather just as much as Lawrence did.

Lawrence had an idea.

"Ah, but the trade guilds will have made arrangements to put their members up for the great market, so I'll inquire with them," he said.

Contacting the trade guild would mean enduring endless questioning about Holo, so Lawrence would have preferred to avoid asking any favors from them, but it didn't seem like that would be possible.

"Oh, you are associated with a trade guild — might I ask which guild?" inquired the merchant.

"The Rowen Trade Guild out of Kumersun."

The young merchant's face brightened instantly. "What a wonderful coincidence! I, too, am a member of the Rowen Guild."

"Ah, surely God has ordained this...Ah, I suppose such talk is taboo here."

"Ha-ha, do not worry. I, too, am a Church follower from the south."

The young merchant smiled, then gave a small, polite cough. "Allow me to introduce myself. I am Fermi Amati, a fish dealer out of Kumersun. I go by Amati in business."

"I'm Kraft Lawrence, a traveling merchant — likewise, I go by Lawrence."

They each sat on their respective wagons, but were nonetheless close enough to shake hands.

Lawrence would now have to introduce Holo.

"This is Holo, my traveling companion. Circumstances have led to her accompanying me, though she is not my wife," said Lawrence with a smile. Holo inclined her head in Amati's direction, looking at him with a small smile.

Holo was quite something when she deigned to be polite.

A flustered Amati reintroduced himself, his cheeks flushed. "Is Miss Holo...a nun?"

"She is a nun on a pilgrimage or something like it, yes."

It wasn't only men whose hearts were stirred into piety; women also regularly went on pilgrimage.

Such women generally introduced themselves as nuns, rather than giving their true identity as townswomen on pilgrimage, since this tended to avoid various troubles.

However, as entering Kumersun dressed in clothes that were instantly recognizable as Church garb presented problems, the custom was to attach three feathers somewhere on the clothing. Holo's cloak indeed had three magnificent, brown chicken feathers pinned to it.

Despite his youth, Amati understood all of this instantly, hailing from the south as he did.

He did not inquire further, reasoning that the young woman probably had a good reason to be traveling with a merchant in such a fashion.

"In any case, the troubles we encounter on our journeys are naught but tests from the heavens. I say this because while I may be able to arrange for a single room, two rooms may unfortunately be difficult," said Amati.

Lawrence seemed taken aback at Amati's statement. Amati smiled and continued, "Surely it is by God's grace that we are of the same trade guild. If I inquire at an inn I've sold fish to, I'm sure I can arrange for a single room. Trying to arrange for a room through the guild will surely lead to all sorts of troublesome questions about your female companion from the old-timers."

"You're quite right, but I don't think we can impose upon you so."

"I'm a businessman, so naturally this is a business proposal. I hope that you will enjoy lots of delicious fish while staying at the inn."

Despite his youth, this Amati with his three wagonloads of fresh fish was clearly a man to be reckoned with.

This was the very image of a shrewd operator.

"You're quite a trader. We'll be happy to take you up on your offer," said Lawrence, half-jealous and half-grateful.

"Understood. Please leave the arrangements to me."

Amati smiled, and for just a moment, his gaze flicked away from Lawrence.

Lawrence pretended not to notice, but Amati had clearly looked at Holo.

It was possible he had been generous not only out of a shrewd business sense, but also from a desire to show his best side to Holo.

For a moment, Lawrence indulged himself in a sense of superiority, as he was the one traveling with Holo, but such silly thoughts would surely bring her ridicule upon him.

He banished the notion from his mind and gave his attention to the task of improving his relationship with the successful young fish merchant before him.

It was only as the sun began to set that they arrived, finally, in Kumersun.

The dinner table was arranged around a bowl of soup made with slices of carp and root vegetables, around which were situated a variety of shellfish dishes.

Amati the fish merchant's presence surely influenced the cuisine, which was quite different from the meat-based meals of the south. It was the steamed snails that stood out the most.

Sea snails were thought to aid longevity, whereas freshwater snails brought only stomach cramps, so they were avoided in the south, where only bivalve shellfish were eaten. The Church even forbade eating snails, claiming that evil spirits inhabited them.

However, that was more practical advice than it was the teachings of God as laid out in scripture. Lawrence himself had long ago become lost, and having arrived at a river, he resorted to eating snails. The memory of the excruciating stomach pain they caused him had made him avoid eating them ever since.

Fortunately the meals were not served in individual portions, and Holo seemed to enjoy the snails greatly.

Lawrence left all the food he couldn't stomach to Holo.

"Hmm. So this is what shellfish tastes like, eh?" said Holo, impressed, as she ate snail after snail, pried free from their shells with a knife Lawrence lent her. For Lawrence's part, he was digging into a salt-broiled river barracuda.

"Don't eat too much, or you'll get a stomachache."

"Mm?"

"Evil spirits live in those river snails. Eat them carelessly, and you'll regret it."

Holo took a quick look at the snail she had just extracted from its shell, then cocked her head, and popped it into her mouth. "Just who do you think I am? It's not just the quality of wheat I can judge."

"Didn't you say something about eating spicy peppers and regretting it?"

Holo seemed to take offense at the reminder.

"Even I can't determine taste purely from appearance. They were bright red, I'll have you know — like a perfectly ripened fruit," said Holo as she extracted yet another snail. Occasionally she would pause to put her cup to her lips and take a drink, closing her eyes as she did so.

Since the region fell outside the Church's baleful eye, distilled liquor — which the Church felt was dangerous — was freely sold and drunk here.

Holo's cup was filled with a nearly transparent liquor known as burnwine.

"Shall I order you something sweeter?"

"......"

Holo shook her head wordlessly, but with her eyes so tightly shut, Lawrence was sure that if he peeked under her robe, he would find her tail fluffed out like a bottlebrush.

At length, she drained the cup, and exhaling deeply, she wiped the corners of her eyes with her sleeve.

Given what she drank (which was also known as "soul-shaking liquor"), it was good that Holo was no longer dressed as a nun. With her head covered by a triangular kerchief, she looked every inch a normal town lass.

Holo had changed clothes before dinner and come to give her regards to Amati once again. Amati's face was so pathetic from Holo's charms that not only Lawrence, but also the innkeeper had been unable to avoid laughing.

As if to add to her burden of sins even more, Holo greeted Amati with even more grace and charm than she normally used.

However, if Amati was to see Holo's ravenous eating and drinking, no doubt he would quickly awaken from his dreams.

Holo sniffed. "'Tis a nostalgic flavor," she said, her eyes a bit teary, either from the liquor or the memories of her homeland.

It was true that the farther north one went, the more common such soul-shaking liquor.

"I can hardly tell any flavor at all when the liquor's been so distilled," said Lawrence.

Perhaps tired of snails, Holo reached for the baked and boiled fish, answering happily as she did so.

"One forgets the sight of something after only ten years, but the taste and the scents linger in the mind for many tens of years longer. This liquor brings back many memories. It's not unlike the liquor of Yoitsu, you know."

"Strong drink is common in the north. Is this all you ever drunk?" Lawrence looked from the contents of the cup to Holo's face.

"Sweeter liquor hardly suits a wisewolf of such noble stature," she answered proudly, a bit of fish clinging to the corner of her mouth.

Of course, based on her appearance, it was sweet milk and honey that would best suit Holo, but Lawrence chuckled and agreed with her.

Surely the taste of the liquor had brought back memories of her homeland.

Holo's happy smile could not be explained away simply by the fact of their first delicious meal in some time.

Hers was the delight of a girl who had received an unexpected gift — the first concrete evidence that they were drawing near to Yoitsu and her home.

21

Yet Lawrence found himself looking away.

It wasn't that he was afraid of his gaze being noticed and of receiving the teasing that would surely follow.

The fact was that he heard Yoitsu had long since been razed to the ground; Lawrence had concealed this from Holo since the beginning of their partnership. Keeping this secret turned Holo's happy smile into a blinding sun too painful to look at.

He couldn't bring himself to destroy the pleasant evening meal.

To avoid Holo noticing his turmoil, Lawrence forcibly turned his thoughts to other things. He smiled at Holo, who reached for the carp stew.

"I see you've taken to the stew?"

"Mm. Who would have guessed that carp, boiled, would be so tasty? Another bowl, please."

The large bowl holding the carp stew was outside Holo's reach, so Lawrence retrieved it for her, but each time he did so, more onions appeared on his wooden plate. It seemed that even boiled, Holo couldn't stand onions.

"Where'd you manage to eat carp? There aren't many places that serve it."

"Hm? I got it from the river. They're sluggish creatures, easy to snare."

Lawrence understood — she'd gone fishing in her wolf form.

"I've never had raw carp. Is it good?" he asked.

"The scales get stuck twixt my teeth, and there are too many bones. I'd seen fish swallow the smaller ones whole and so imagined them to be delicious, but in the end, they did not suit me."

Lawrence imagined Holo's huge form as she wolfed down a large carp headfirst.

Carp were renowned for their long life and were both revered as holy and reviled as tools of the devil by the Church. For that reason, the eating of carp was confined to the north.

To be fair, it seemed mildly ridiculous to hold the carp, with its moderate longevity, in such esteem when there were wolves like Holo wandering about.

"Human cooking is indeed good, but it's not just that — the fish was chosen very well. That Amati lad has quite an eye."

"For his age, yes. And that was quite a load he was moving."

"And on the other hand, there's you. What was it you're hauling, again?" Holo's eyes were suddenly cold.

"Hm? Nails. Like this table . . . Oh, I guess it doesn't use them."

"I know what nails are. I'm saying you should've gone for something a bit more impressive. Or are you still reeling from your failure in Ruvinheigen?"

Lawrence felt rather aggrieved by this, but it was the truth, and so he could say nothing.

He had become overenthusiastic and bought armor on margin that amounted to roughly twice his personal net worth, and as a result, he had faced bankruptcy and lifelong slavery. In addition, he had caused Holo significant trouble and humiliation.

Having been humbled, Lawrence chose to buy simple nails on his way out of Ruvinheigen, to the tune of about four hundred silver *trenni*. It was a conservative purchase that left him with quite a bit of cash on hand.

"It may not be the grandest load, but it should turn a fair profit. And it's not as though there's nothing attractive in my wagon."

Holo cocked her head at Lawrence, holding a river barracuda in her mouth as though she were an alley cat.

Lawrence had come up with a nice bon mot.

He coughed slightly. "I mean, you're riding in it as well, after all."

It was a bit affected, but Lawrence flattered himself to think that it was a charming line nonetheless.

As he smiled, took a drink of his burnwine, and looked to Holo, he saw that she had stopped moving and seemed quite at a loss.

"...Well, I suppose that's about all you're capable of," she finally said with a sigh.

"You know, it wouldn't kill you to be a little nicer to me," said Lawrence.

"Ah, but if you treat a male too well, he'll soon come to expect it all the time. And then you'll hear naught but the same foolish words over and over."

"Ugh..." Lawrence couldn't let this slight go unanswered. "Fine, then. From now on I'll—"

"You dunce," said Holo, cutting him off. "How precious do you think a male's kindness is?"

"......" Lawrence frowned and escaped into his drink, but Holo was on the hunt now.

"And all I need do for your kindness is to seem downcast, nay?"

Her innocent face accused him, and Lawrence had no response.

Holo was unfair.

He looked at her, resentful, but she only smiled pleasantly.

Having finished their first proper meal in many days, Holo and Lawrence returned to their inn, where the streets were quiet.

They had arrived in Kumersun around sunset, but the streets had been much more congested than Lawrence anticipated.

If they hadn't encountered Amati, they certainly would have had to prevail upon the trade guild for a room and might even have wound up staying in a room at the guild house itself.

All around the city, wooden carvings and wheat dolls, whose inspiration was unclear, lined the streets, with bands and jesters flooding even the narrowest of alleyways.

The great market that took place in the large plaza in the south end of the city had its hours extended, and it bustled with an energy that befit the word *festival*. Even craftsmen who were normally not allowed to sell their wares here had stalls set up along the wide street.

Back in the inn, Lawrence opened the window to cool his body, still flushed from the strong liquor. He could yet see some shopkeepers tidying up their stalls, illuminated by moonlight.

The room that Amati had arranged for them was in one of the very finest inns in the town, one that Lawrence would never have considered staying at himself. The room was on the second floor, overlooking the wide street that ran from north to south through the center of the city, not far from the intersection with the street's east-west counterpart. Just as Holo had hoped, it had two beds. Of course, Lawrence could not help harboring a suspicion that the two beds of the room were also due to Amati's insistence.

It mollified Lawrence to think this, but he was still grateful for Amati's assistance, so he abandoned that train of thought and looked out onto the street.

Everybody on the wide boulevard seemed to be staggering home.

Lawrence chuckled and looked behind him to see Holo sitting cross-legged on the bed, pouring herself another cup of wine as if she hadn't already had enough to drink.

"Don't come crying to me if you're hungover tomorrow. Have you already forgotten what happened in Pazzio?"

"Mm? Oh, this is fine. Fine liquor never lingers past its welcome. And who am I to turn down its friendship?"

Now finished pouring, she happily put the cup to her lips, then ate a bit of dried trout left over from dinner.

Left to her own devices, Holo would most likely eat and drink herself into a stupor, but Lawrence was still grateful for her pleasant mood.

He had to broach a subject that was far from his favorite.

The reason he had altered his usual yearly route, which included Kumersun only in the summer months, was because he was heading for Holo's homeland.

Lawrence was not clear on precisely where Holo's home of Yoitsu was. Although he had heard of its name, that was in a story from ancient times, which provided no concrete sense of its location.

He had avoided pressing her for more information thus far, because every time the subject came up, she would smile with nostalgia but soon sink into a depression at the realization of the distance, both temporal and spatial, that separated her from home.

As sad as it was, that was reason enough for him to hesitate to bring up Yoitsu.

But if Lawrence were to mention it now that they were closer, there would be nothing to be sad about, he decided. He sat on the desk that was placed against one wall and spoke.

"So, before you're three sheets to the wind, there's something I want to ask you."

Holo's exposed ears immediately pricked up.

Her gaze soon followed. "What might that be?"

Evidently her keen wolf senses had already picked up that Lawrence was not engaging in idle banter. A thin smile curled her lips, a sure sign of her good mood.

Lawrence forced the words out of his mouth. "It's about your home village."

Holo immediately grinned and took another sip.

This was odd; Lawrence had expected her to turn serious at the mention of Yoitsu.

Just as he concluded that she must already be drunk, Holo swallowed her wine and spoke.

"So you don't know where it is, eh? I was starting to wonder when you were going to ask." Then looking down as if gazing at the reflection of her smile in the wine, Holo said, "Do you really think I go to pieces at every mention of Yoitsu? Do I seem so weak?"

Lawrence considered mentioning the time she had cried over a dream of her homeland, but Holo was certainly aware of this. Her tail wagged happily.

"Not at all," said Lawrence.

"Fool. That was your chance to say 'Aye, you do!'"

Her tail flicked once, as if she had received the answer she actually wanted.

"Still, you do worry over the strangest things. So you decided to finally bring this up now, after seeing my mood at supper? Such a soft touch." She giggled as she drank her wine, then continued, "I can't say it doesn't make me happy, though it's mostly your foolishness that is so amusing. Did you plan on getting lost in the northlands before finally asking me?"

Lawrence shrugged. "Will you tell me where Yoitsu is, so I don't look any more foolish than I have to?"

Holo paused, taking a sip from her cup.

She gave a long sigh.

"I do not exactly remember."

She continued, as if to preempt Lawrence's imminent protest that she had to have been joking.

"I know the direction, certainly. It is that way."

Lawrence looked in the direction she pointed, which was obviously north.

"But I do not remember how many mountains to cross, nor how many rivers, nor how long one most walk across the plains. I had thought I would remember as we get closer—will that not do?"

"Can't you even give me a hint as to where it might be? The path is not a straight one, and once we arrive in the north country, maps will be hard to come by. Depending on the location, the path could be very roundabout. Do you remember the names of any nearby places, for example?"

Holo pondered this for a moment, a finger pressed to her temple. "I remember Yoitsu and Nyohhira. And…hmm…What was it…Pi—"

"Pi?"

"Pire…no, Piro…That's right! Pirohmoten."

Holo seemed quite happy to have recalled the name, but Lawrence only cocked his head. "I haven't heard of that place. Is there anything else?"

"Er…there were many towns, but they didn't all have names the way towns do now. One could just point and say a town was beyond that mountain, and that was enough. We didn't need names."

It was true; Lawrence had been surprised by this the first time he visited the north. He had arrived at a certain town and found that its name was used only by travelers. Neither its residents nor the people living nearby knew or cared about the town's name.

There were elderly people who claimed that naming a town would bring it to the attention of evil spirits.

Undoubtedly what they really meant by "evil spirits" was the Church.

"Well, we'll start at Nyohhira, then. I know where that is."

"That name brings back such memories. Are the hot springs still there?"

"I've heard that nobles and bishops secretly visit the town for its hot springs, despite the fact that it's in pagan lands. According to rumor, it's even exempt from Church attacks because of those same hot springs."

"Those springs don't belong to any one group, after all," said

Holo before coughing slightly. "If Nyohhira's our goal, then from Nyohhira it is that way."

Holo pointed southwest — not north to Lawrence's relief.

Any farther north than Nyohhira meant lands where the snow never melted, even in the summer.

Yet even knowing that Yoitsu was southwest of Nyohhira left too wide a region.

"How long did it take to get from Nyohhira to Yoitsu?"

"For me, two days. For a human...I do not know."

Lawrence thought back to the time he had ridden on Holo's back when she was in wolf form, near Ruvinheigen. She would have no trouble traversing unimproved roads.

That left too much area to search, even starting from Nyohhira. Searching for a town that itself might only be a tiny village would be like looking for a needle in a desert. It was precisely because Lawrence himself was a traveling merchant, who was used to walking from town to town, that he understood the difficulty involved.

There was also still the fact that Lawrence had heard Yoitsu had been destroyed by a great bear spirit.

If that was true, finding the remains of a town that had been destroyed centuries earlier would be truly impossible.

Lawrence was not a nobleman with the luxury of passing his days in idleness. He could only stray from his original trade route for six months at the outside. His mistake in Ruvinheigen had set him still further back from his goal of opening a shop, and he did not have anything like a surplus of free time.

He was thinking all this over when something finally occurred to him.

"Could you not find it yourself from Nyohhira? You know the general direction, right?"

If it was just two days from Nyohhira, then just as Holo said, she would most likely be able to remember the details as she got closer.

The words had simply fallen from his mouth without any particular ill intent, but no sooner had Lawrence spoken than he realized his mistake.

Holo looked at him, stunned.

Surprise also registered on Lawrence's face as Holo looked away.

"Y-yes...if I got as far as Nyohhira, I could certainly find my way to Yoitsu."

Holo forced a smile. Lawrence wondered what was wrong, then voiced a sudden "Ah —" as the realization dawned.

In the port town of Pazzio, Holo had said that loneliness was a deathly illness.

Holo feared loneliness above all else. Even if he didn't mean anything by it, she was likely to take his suggestion hard, and she had been drinking.

She probably took his suggestion to mean that he had grown weary of searching for her homeland.

"Hey, now, wait just a minute. Don't take it the wrong way. There's no reason I couldn't wait in Nyohhira while you searched for a couple of days."

"Yes. That would be enough. You'll guide me as far as Nyohhira, won't you? I had hoped to see a few more towns."

The conversation moved so smoothly it was almost a letdown, and Lawrence had to attribute this to Holo's agile mind.

Despite her apparent agreeability, a disconnect lay beneath it.

Holo had been away from her homeland for centuries. Just as in the legend Lawrence had heard, she had to have considered the possibility that Yoitsu no longer existed, and even if it did, the countless months and years would have wrought great changes. She must have been filled with uncertainty.

No doubt she was afraid of going to her homeland alone.

That uncertainty was disguised by Holo's innocent, happy smile when she claimed the liquor reminded her of Yoitsu.

A few moments' thought made this clear, and Lawrence regretted his rash suggestion.

"Listen, I have every intention of helping you as much as I can. What I said before —"

"Didn't I ask before how precious a male's kindness was? I can't have you being too kind."

Holo's forced smile mixed with her troubled expression as she set her cup down on the bed and continued, "I'm in the wrong. I can't help thinking of things from my own perspective. But you humans, you become old in what seems like the blink of an eye to me. I always forget how precious a single year is for someone with such a brief life span."

The moonlight streamed in through the room's large window, illuminating Holo. She seemed almost unreal to Lawrence in that moment; he hesitated to approach her for fear that she would disappear.

Holo looked up after staring into the contents of her cup, still with that same troubled smile.

"You really are too softhearted. What am I to do with you when you look at me so?"

What was the right thing to say? Lawrence could not find the words he wanted.

A rift had undeniably formed between the two of them.

Yet the words to heal it would not come. A convenient lie would be useless as Holo would see through it instantly.

Holo's words had made it hard for Lawrence to say anything at all. He couldn't very well tell her he would see her through to Yoitsu no matter how many years it took. Merchants were too practical by far for such grandiosity. The many centuries of Holo's life were too distant.

"I am the one who lost sight of the obvious. I have gotten too comfortable by your side. I presumed...too much," said Holo with a self-conscious smile, her ears twitching with her embarrassment. She spoke like a maiden from somewhere near the bottom of her heart.

But such honesty did not bring Lawrence any pleasure.

It was as though Holo was saying good-bye.

"Heh, I seem to be a bit drunk. I'd better sleep, or who knows what I'll wind up saying."

Holo was never reticent at the best of times, but the way she talked made it seem like she was simply putting on a brave face.

In the end, Lawrence was unable to say anything to her.

All he could do was take note of the fact that she had not yet simply packed up and left. It seemed simultaneously unthinkable and entirely likely that she would do such a thing.

Lawrence wanted to scream at himself for being so powerless to help her.

The night silently deepened.

The cries of drunken revelers could be heard from beyond the window.

CHAPTER TWO

No matter how plagued with worry merchants may be, it is said that they always manage to sleep well.

So it was that despite Lawrence's concern that Holo might depart on her own during the night, Lawrence slept soundly and awoke to birdsong coming in through the window.

He didn't do anything so flagrant as jumping frantically out of bed, but Lawrence did glance at the bed next to his and sighed in relief when he saw that Holo was still there.

He got out of bed to look outside the window. It was quite cold within the room, but the early-morning air outside was still colder; his breath turned smoke white in it.

Yet the cold air was perfectly clear — a morning made of crystal.

There were already people on the street that the inn faced. Looking down at the town merchants, who rose still earlier than the notoriously early-rising traveling merchants, Lawrence arranged the day's plans in his mind, finally saying "all right" to himself when they were in order.

Though it would not exactly compensate for the previous night's blunder, Lawrence wanted to be able to fully enjoy the festival — which started the next day — with Holo, and that meant concluding his business today.

The first order of business would be selling the merchandise he'd gotten in Ruvinheigen, he thought to himself as he turned around to look back at the room.

Still a bit heavyhearted from the previous evening, Lawrence walked over to his companion, who slumbered away as usual, intending to wake her — when he stopped and furrowed his brows.

It wasn't unusual for Holo to sleep as late as she pleased, but something else was amiss.

Her usual guileless snoring was entirely absent.

Lawrence wondered if the silence was what he thought it was, reaching out to her. She seemed to sense it; the blanket stirred minutely.

He lifted the covers up gently.

What he saw made him sigh.

Holo's face beneath the covers was more pathetic than any abandoned kitten.

"Hungover again, eh?"

Her ears twitched slightly; perhaps it hurt too much to move her head.

He thought about teasing Holo about it but remembered the previous night and thought better of it. And in any case, she would be in no mood to listen.

"I'll bring a cup of water and a bucket just in case. You just be good and rest."

He put extra emphasis on the "be good" part, which her ears twitched at yet again.

Lawrence didn't think she would behave just because he told her to, but she was unlikely to go wandering off in her current state. Given the impossibility of her packing up and striking off on her own, he let himself relax a bit.

He knew Holo was fully capable of faking a hangover, but her face had been so pale he doubted this one was fake.

Turning the thoughts over in his head, he finished his preparations for going out without saying another word and then came back to her bedside — she was evidently incapable of so much as turning herself over.

"The festival doesn't get going until tomorrow, so you needn't rush yourself."

Relief showed instantly on Holo's exhausted, alcohol-ravaged face; Lawrence had to laugh.

It seemed that even suffering a hangover was less important to Holo than attending the festival.

"I'll be back in the afternoon."

Holo's ears were still; this statement did not interest her.

Lawrence gave a strained smile, at which point the corners of Holo's mouth curled ever so slowly into a grin.

She seemed to be doing it on purpose.

Lawrence slumped over and drew the covers back over Holo. She was undoubtedly still grinning away under there.

Still, he was genuinely relieved that she seemed not to hold a grudge from the previous night.

As he left the room, Lawrence took one more look back at Holo. Her tail stuck out from underneath the blanket, and it flicked twice, as if waving good-bye.

Thinking he would buy her something tasty, he closed the door behind him.

Trying to do business before the ring of the bell that opens a market is not generally smiled upon in any town — and this is even truer when one is smack-dab in the middle of the marketplace.

However, depending on the time and circumstances, this rule can be bent.

In Kumersun it was even half-encouraged to mitigate the congestion that came with the opening of the market during the festival.

So despite the early hour, with the sun just beginning to rise above the buildings, the marketplace—which took up half of Kumersun's southern plaza—was already busy with merchants.

Here and there were stacks of crates and piles of burlap sacks, and pigs, chickens, and all manner of livestock stood tied up or caged in the cramped spaces between goods and the stalls. As Kumersun was the largest exporter of fish in the landlocked region, it was easy to spot fish swimming in huge barrels of freshwater, not unlike the ones Amati had been hauling the previous day.

Just as Holo was unable to hide her excitement when faced with a line of eateries, Lawrence's pulse could not help but quicken when he saw the vast array of goods in the marketplace.

How much profit could one make transporting this good to that town? This other commodity was so plentiful that there must be a surplus of it in that location—would the price be lower? Such thoughts chased each other through Lawrence's mind.

When he was just starting out as a merchant, Lawrence had no sense of what was a favorable price for a good, so he wandered about aimlessly without knowing what to do—but now he could discern all kinds of things.

Once a merchant fully grasped this intricate web of commodities, he became like an alchemist, transmuting lead into gold.

Lawrence felt giddy at the power this notion afforded him until he remembered his failure in Ruvinheigen, which he chuckled at, chagrined.

Turning one's eyes to avarice made it all the more easy to stumble, after all.

He took a breath to calm himself, grasping the reins and heading into the center of the marketplace. The stall he finally arrived at was already well into its business day, like all the others. The shop's owner was just a year removed from Lawrence and had also started out as a traveling merchant. The fact that he had become a proper wheat merchant — complete with stall, which despite its small size even had a proper roof — was generally attributed to the man's good fortune. He had even adopted the squarish facial hair style that was common in the region.

Said wheat merchant — Mark Cole — was momentarily surprised upon seeing Lawrence, but he immediately composed himself and raised a hand in greeting, smiling.

The other merchant that Mark dealt with turned to regard Lawrence as well, nodding in greeting. One never knew when he might encounter someone who could become a business partner, so Lawrence flashed his best merchant's smile and gestured at them to by all means please continue their conversation.

"*Le, spandi amirto. Vanderji.*"

"*Ha-ha. Pireji. Bao!*"

Evidently their exchange was just ending; the man spoke to Mark in a language Lawrence didn't understand and then took his leave. Naturally, Lawrence did not forget to give the man another professional smile as he left.

He committed the man's face to memory in case they were to meet again in some other town.

These were the tiny interactions that accumulated over time, eventually turning into profit.

The merchant — who was probably from somewhere in the northlands — disappeared into the crowds, and Lawrence finally descended from his wagon.

"I guess I interrupted your business."

"Hardly! He was just talking my ear off about how grateful he was to the god of Pitra Mountain. You saved me," said Mark, rolling up a sheet of parchment as he sat atop a wooden chest. He smiled at the tedium of the man's conversation.

Mark, like Lawrence, was a member of the Rowen Trade Guild. Their acquaintance was the result of showing up every year in the same marketplace to trade, and the two had known each other since the very beginning of their respective careers. They could easily skip the usual formalities.

"If I'd known better, I wouldn't have bothered learning their language. They're not bad men, but once they figure out you can understand them, you'll never hear the end of how great their god is."

"Might be that a local deity's still better than a god who never leaves the shrine except when they spy a flash of gold, eh?" Lawrence said.

Mark laughed, tapping his own head with the now rolled-up parchment. "You're not lying! And they say harvest gods are all beautiful women."

Holo's face appeared in Lawrence's mind. He nodded and grinned but of course did not say what sprang to mind: *But they have terrible personalities.*

"Anyway, enough of such talk. I'll be scolded by the missus for sure. Shall we talk of trade? I presume that's why you're here."

Mark's expression shifted from friendly banter to business. Though there was no need for formalities between the two, their relationship was a calculated one. Lawrence readied himself for the exchange and spoke.

"I've brought nails from Ruvinheigen. Thought you might want to buy them up."

"Nails, eh? I'm a wheat seller. Did you hear somewhere that we now nail our sacks of wheat closed? I think not."

"Ah, but you'll soon have many customers laying in supplies for the long winter. You could sell those nails just as you sell the wheat. People need them to brace up their homes against the snow."

Mark looked skyward for a moment before rolling his gaze back to Lawrence.

"I suppose that is true...Nails, you say. How many?"

"I've one hundred twenty nails of three *paté* in length, two hundred in four *paté*, and two hundred in five *paté*, along with a statement of quality from the Ruvinheigen blacksmiths' guild."

Mark scratched his cheek with one end of the rolled-up parchment and sighed. This feigned reluctance was a common merchant trait.

"I'll take the lot for ten and a half *lumione*."

"What's the *lumione* trading at now? Against trenni silver."

"Thirty-four even when yesterday's market closed. So that'd be...three hundred fifty-seven *trenni*."

"Too low by far, sir," said Lawrence.

The amount wasn't even as much as Lawrence had spent to buy the nails. Mark's brow furrowed at Lawrence's quick answer.

"Have you heard about the crash in armor prices?" Mark asked. "With no military expeditions into the north this year, people are unloading armor and swords left and right, which means there's a glut of raw iron. Even nails are cheaper now — even ten *lumione* is a generous price."

It was the response he had expected, so Lawrence calmed himself and replied.

"Aye, but that's in the south. When there's so much iron to be melted down, the price of fuel will rise enough to make it impractical. If you can buy enough firewood to melt iron this time of the year in Ploania, I'd sure like to see it. Anybody that tries it is likely to have their head split with a kindling ax."

Once winter came to regions with a lot of snow, the supply of firewood stagnated. The iron forges, with their bottomless appetite for fuel, were abandoned during the winter. If some blacksmith did decide to forge in the winter, the price of firewood would immediately skyrocket, and he would soon find himself showered in the curses of the shivering townspeople. Thus, even if the raw material for nails was suddenly abundant in the region, the original price of those nails should hold steady.

Any merchant with a bit of experience would be able to put this much together.

Unsurprisingly, Mark grinned. "Come now, must you be selling nails to a poor wheat merchant? If it's grain, then sure, I know how to buy it cheap, but nails are far from my specialty."

"Sixteen *lumione*, then."

"Too dear. Thirteen."

"Fifteen."

"Fourteen and two-thirds." Mark's medium frame stiffened, leaving him loglike.

Lawrence could tell he would get no further in his negotiations.

Pushing it would only damage the business relationship. Lawrence nodded and extended his right hand. "It's done, then."

"Well met, guild brother!" said Mark with a smile, shaking Lawrence's hand.

The price was undoubtedly quite a compromise on Mark's end, as well.

As a wheat merchant, Mark was not, strictly speaking, even allowed to buy or sell nails. Which merchant could sell what good was decided by the respective guilds, so to stock a new item, a merchant had to either obtain the permission of the other merchants already selling that item or cut them in on the profits.

At a glance, this rule would seem to obstruct free trade, but if it was absent, giant companies with huge amounts of capital would soon swallow the entire marketplace. The rule was designed to prevent that from happening.

"Would you prefer to settle up in coin or credit?" asked Mark.

"Credit, if you please."

"Thank goodness. There are so many cash deals this time of year it's hard to keep up."

While traders had no trouble keeping track of their deals in their ledger books, plenty of people bringing goods into the villages and towns would want coin and only coin.

But currency shortages were serious problems in any town. Even if a merchant had assets to buy a particular good, without the currency to make the payment, there could be no commerce at all. And an illiterate farmer wouldn't even blow his nose on a promissory note.

In the wilderness, it was the knight with his sword who was strongest, but in the cities, coin equaled power. This was why the Church had grown so wealthy. Collecting tithes week after week, it could not help but become powerful.

"So since I'm taking credit, I've got a favor to ask of you," said Lawrence as Mark approached to unload the sack of nails from the wagon bed. The wheat merchant's face grew instantly wary.

"It's nothing terribly important. I've got to head north to take care of something, and I wondered if you'd ask after the conditions of the roads and passes up that way. Your customer before me, he was from the north, no?"

Seeing that Lawrence's question had nothing to do with business, Mark visibly relaxed.

His shift in expression was obviously intentional, Lawrence noted with chagrin. It was probably Mark's way of getting back at Lawrence a bit for selling the nails so dear.

"Aye, that's easy enough," said Mark. "Though it would've been easier for you to come in the summertime as you normally do. Must be something pretty big to get you heading up north in midwinter."

"Well, you know, this and that. I will say it's nothing to do with business, though."

"Ha-ha-ha. Even the ever-traveling merchant can't free himself from life's little obligations, eh? So where are you headed?"

"A place called Yoitsu. Heard of it?"

Mark leaned on the cart as he raised a single eyebrow. "Can't say I have. But who knows how many little towns and villages I've never heard of. You want me to find someone who knows it, then?"

"Well, in any case, we're heading for Nyohhira, so you can ask about Yoitsu sort of 'by the way'; that'll be fine."

"Right, then. So if you're bound for Nyohhira you'll be crossing the Dolan Plains."

"You know the way, then? That makes it easier for me."

The wheat merchant nodded and thumped his chest, as if to say "leave it to me." Mark would surely be able to collect the information Lawrence needed.

This was exactly why Lawrence had come to Mark in the first place, but if he had interrupted the wheat merchant during this most busy of seasons simply to gather information without bringing some business along as well, it would have weighed on his conscience — and Mark would've been none too pleased.

That is why he brought the nails to sell. Lawrence was well aware that Mark knew many of the area blacksmiths. It would be easy for Mark to sell off the nails to any of them for a tidy profit.

Mark would even be able to ask for a portion of the payment for those nails in cash. As a wheat merchant — for whom the last chance to save up money was rapidly approaching — the chance to get a bit of hard coin into his hands would probably make him happier than any meager profit.

And as Lawrence had expected, Mark readily agreed. That took care of the need to gather information on the upcoming travel.

"Oh, yes. There was another thing I wanted to ask you about. Don't worry, this will be quick," said Lawrence.

"Do I look *that* stingy?"

Lawrence met Mark's chagrined smile. "Does this town have any chroniclers?"

"Chroniclers…? Oh, you mean the people who write those endless diaries of town events?"

Chroniclers were paid a retainer by nobles or Church officials and kept histories of a given area or town.

Lawrence couldn't help but laugh at hearing Mark dismiss their work as "endless diaries."

It wasn't entirely accurate, but nor was it far from the truth, which made it all the funnier.

"I don't think they'd like you putting it that way, but yes," Lawrence said.

"Bah, it just bothers me that all they need do to earn coin is sit in a chair all day and write."

"That's a little hard to take from someone who got so lucky in a deal he was able to open a shop in a town."

The story of Mark's good fortune was a famous one.

Lawrence laughed again, this time at Mark's momentarily stunned expression.

"So, are there any chroniclers or nay?"

"Ah…yes, I think there are. But I wouldn't get mixed up with them were I you," said Mark, taking hold of the bag of nails in Lawrence's wagon. "Rumor has it one was accused of heresy by a monastery somewhere and had to flee. The town's filled with people like that who had to run."

The townspeople of Kumersun were less concerned with the animosity between pagans and the Church than they were with economic prosperity, so the town had naturally become a refuge for a variety of naturalists, philosophers, and other such heretics.

"I just have some things I want to ask after," said Lawrence. "Chroniclers collect local legends and such, yes? I've an interest in such matters."

"Now, why would you care about that? Do you need conversation starters for when you travel north?"

"Something like that. I know it's sudden, but do you think you might introduce me to one?"

Mark turned his head slightly and called out toward his stand, with the bag of nails still in one hand.

A boy emerged from behind a mountain of wheat sacks. Evidently Mark had reached a point where he could have an apprentice.

"I do know one. Better if it's someone from Rowen, right?" said Mark, handing bag after bag of nails to his young apprentice.

Seeing this, Lawrence was filled with a renewed sense of urgency to get to Yoitsu and return to his normal business routine as quickly as he could.

Yet it would be trouble if Holo discerned that fact — and for his part, it was not as though Lawrence wished to be rid of her.

He found it impossible to reconcile his two feelings on the issue.

If he lived as long as Holo did, taking a year or two off from business would hardly be an issue.

But Lawrence's life was too short for that.

"What's the matter?"

"Hm? Oh…nothing. Yes, if there's a chronicler in the trade guild, that would be convenient. Can I ask you to introduce me?"

"I can certainly do that much, yes. I'll even do it for free."

Lawrence couldn't help but smile at the effort Mark put into saying "free."

"Is sooner better?" asked Mark.

"If possible, yes."

"I'll send the boy out, then. There's a fearless old peddler named

Gi Batos there, and if I'm remembering right, he's close with a pagan hermit who's done chronicle work. Old Batos takes the week before and after the festival off, so if you go by the guild house around midday, you should find him drinking the day away."

Even within a single guild, such as Rowen Trade Guild, traveling merchants like Lawrence might not know many others within it—like Amati whose business was unrelated to Lawrence's own.

Lawrence repeated Gi Batos's name to himself, carving it into his memory.

"Understood. I'm in your debt."

"Ha-ha. If that's all it takes to be in my debt, I'd hate to think what comes next. Enough of that talk—you'll be in town until the festival ends, yes? Stop by for a drink, won't you?"

"I suppose I should let you brag of your success at least once. I'll be by."

Mark raised his voice in a laugh and then sighed as he handed the last bag of nails to his apprentice. "Even a town merchant endures endless troubles and worries, though. Sometimes I wish I could go back to traveling."

Lawrence could only smile in vague agreement as he was still toiling day in and day out to achieve what Mark already had. Mark seemed to realize this. "Uh, forget I said that," he said, smiling apologetically.

"All we can do is keep our noses to the grindstone. It's the same for all merchants."

"True enough. Good fortune to the both of us, then!"

Lawrence shook hands with Mark, and after seeing another customer come to call on the wheat merchant, he put the stall behind him.

He slowly maneuvered his wagon into the crowd and then looked back at Mark's stand.

There stood Mark, who seemed to have forgotten about Lawrence entirely and was now embroiled in negotiations with his next customer. Lawrence was frankly envious.

But even Mark the successful town merchant said he sometimes wished to return to traveling.

Lawrence remembered a story. Long ago, there was a king who planned to alleviate the poverty in his own kingdom by invading the prosperous nation next to his own, but a court poet had said this: "One always sees the wretched parts of one's own land and the best parts of one's neighbor's."

Lawrence thought on the story.

He had been focusing on the troubles involved in finding Holo's homeland or the setbacks he'd suffered in Ruvinheigen, but the fact was he had been able to travel with a companion of rare quality.

If Lawrence had never encountered Holo, he would have continued along his usual trade route, enduring the endless loneliness that came with it.

It had once been so bad that he started to seriously fantasize about what it would be like if his horse became human. As he pondered this, Lawrence realized that one of his dreams had already come true.

There was a good chance that eventually he would be traveling alone again, and when that time came, Lawrence knew he would look back on this time with Holo with no shortage of fondness.

Lawrence gripped the reins once again.

Once he finished making the rounds through the trade guilds and merchant firms, he would make sure to buy a truly delicious lunch for Holo.

Kumersun lacked a church, so it was a bell tower atop the highest roof of the tallest noble house in town that grandly rang the noontime bell each day. The bell, of course, was decorated with carvings of the finest sort, and the roof, visible throughout the entire town, was maintained by the finest artisans that could be had.

It was said that the roof — constructed solely because of the vanity of the nobility it housed — had cost fully three hundred *lumione*, but the people of the town bore the nobles no ill will, reasoning that it was doing such things that made one nobility.

Perhaps the reason most wealthy merchants, who hoarded their money in great vaults, were so richly resented was because they lacked that playful sense of extravagance. Even the most famously violent of knights would be beloved if he spent freely enough.

Lawrence thought on this as he opened the door to his room — and was struck face on by the sharp tang of liquor.

"So it smelled this bad, did it..."

Lawrence suddenly regretted not rinsing his mouth before venturing out, but the greater part of the smell was surely the fault of the wolf that even now slept before him.

Holo showed no signs of stirring even when Lawrence entered the room, but her artless snoring suggested that she had mostly recovered from her hangover.

The stink of liquor was too much for Lawrence, so he opened the window before approaching the bed. The water glass next to it was empty as was — fortunately — the bucket. Her face, sticking out of the bedclothes, looked haler than it had before. Lawrence had bought real wheat bread, which he rarely indulged in, instead of honeyed crackers; this had been the right choice, he felt.

He was quite sure that the first words out of Holo's mouth upon awaking would be "I'm hungry."

Lawrence held the bag of bread up to Holo's nose, which twitched slightly. Unlike the tough, bitter oat and rye bread they often wound up eating, the scent of the soft, tender wheat bread was wholly enticing.

Holo's sniffing at the bag was enough to make Lawrence doubt whether she was actually asleep. At length, she made a small, artless *mmph* sound and then buried her face within the covers.

Lawrence looked down at the foot of the bed, where he saw Holo's tail sticking out of the covers, trembling slightly.

She seemed to be in mid yawn there beneath the bedclothes.

Lawrence waited a spell, and sure enough, Holo's bleary-eyed face eventually emerged from underneath the covers.

"Mmph…Something smells amazing…"

"Feeling better?"

Holo rubbed her eyes, yawned again, and spoke as if to herself. "I'm hungry."

Despite his best efforts not to, Lawrence burst out laughing.

Not seeming particularly interested, Holo slowly hauled herself up and yawned a third time. She then sniffed the air and turned her gluttonous gaze to the bag Lawrence held.

"I figured you'd say that. I splurged and got some wheat bread."

As soon as Lawrence handed over the bag, the proud wisewolf became like a cat presented with a treat.

"Will you not eat some?"

Holo sat there on the bed, clutching the bag and devouring the pure white bread, looking anything but willing to share.

Even as she posed the question to him, her mien was now closer to that of a hunting dog who had no intention of letting its prey escape.

It was probably at the limits of Holo's generosity to even venture to ask him before she finished the entire bag.

"No, I'm fine. I had a taste earlier."

Normally she would have regarded him with some suspicion, but Holo — true to her ability to see right through a lie — seemed to accept this as the truth. Visibly relieved, she returned to her assault on the bread.

"Careful, you'll choke."

Lawrence remembered when shortly after he and Holo first met, she nearly choked on some potatoes at the small church they had passed the night in. She shot him a glare, which he chuckled at. He pulled a chair out from the desk and sat.

Upon the desk were several wax-sealed envelopes. After making the rounds among the various trading firms, Lawrence had received several letters addressed to him.

Despite their itinerant lifestyle, traveling merchants had many opportunities to send and receive letters as their seasonal stops were very predictable.

Some offered to buy a certain good at a high price if they happened to be passing through a given town that was selling it; others told of a good's price in their towns and asked how it was doing elsewhere — the correspondence was diverse.

Yet it was strange, Lawrence felt. He generally came through Kumersun in the summertime, so it was out of the ordinary for letters to be reaching him here now on the very threshold of winter. In the worst case, the letters would have wound up languishing in the files of the trading companies for more than half a year. If the letters had not found Lawrence in Kumersun within two weeks, they were to be sent south. It went without saying that such arrangements cost a pretty penny.

It was clear that the letters were urgent.

The senders were all town merchants situated in northern Ploania.

Lawrence carefully removed the wax seals with a knife when he sensed Holo peering intently at him.

"They're letters."

"Mm," came Holo's short reply as she sat herself on the desk, bread in hand.

Lawrence didn't mind if she saw the envelope's contents, so after breaking the seal, he took the letter out right there on the spot.

"Dear Mr. Lawrence..."

The fact that the letter did not begin with "In the name of our Lord" was very much in keeping with a northerner's style.

Lawrence skimmed the pleasantries and moved his gaze down the page.

Following the messy, hurriedly composed handwriting, he quickly discerned the letter's import.

It was indeed critical information for a merchant to have.

He read the second letter, confirming that its contents were the same as the first, and then sighed, smiling slightly.

"What do they say?" Holo asked.

"Care to take a guess?"

Perhaps irritated at having her question answered with another question, Holo frowned and rolled her eyes. "They hardly seem like love letters."

Even a love of a hundred years would find its ardor cooled by such messy handwriting, Lawrence thought.

He handed the letters to Holo and grinned. "You always get important information *after* you most need it."

"Hmph."

"These letters were sent out of sincere concern, so I owe them some gratitude at least. What think you?"

Holo licked her fingers, either out of contentment or because she had simply eaten all there was to eat, and looked at the letters she held in the other hand.

She then shoved them back at Lawrence, a sour expression on her face.

"I cannot read."

"Oh...you can't?"

Lawrence took the letters, and Holo narrowed her eyes at him.

"If you're feigning ignorance, I must say you're getting better at it."

"No, no, sorry. I really had no idea."

Holo regarded him for a moment as if to ascertain the truth of his words, and then she turned away with a sigh.

"First of all," she said, "there are too many letters to remember and too many baffling combinations. You might say all one needs to do is write as one would speak, but that is clearly a lie."

It seemed Holo had once tried to learn to read.

"You mean the consonant notation and such?"

"I've no idea what you call them, but the rules are too complex by far. If there's one way in which you humans exceed us wolves, it is your mastery of those inexplicable symbols."

Lawrence very nearly asked if other wolves were similarly unable to write, but he swallowed the question at the last second, merely nodding his agreement.

"Though it's not as if it's a simple matter for us to memorize them, either," he said. "I had no easy time of it, and every time I made a mistake, my teacher would strike me on the head for it. I thought I'd have a permanent lump."

Holo regarded him dubiously. If she thought he was merely humoring her, she would undoubtedly become angry.

"Surely you can tell I'm not lying," said Lawrence.

Holo finally turned her doubtful gaze away. "So what is it that's written there?"

"Ah, it says that the northern campaigns have been canceled, so be careful of buying up armor," Lawrence said, tossing the letters aside. He grinned ruefully at Holo's blank look.

"So if you had but received that letter sooner, you wouldn't have gotten in trouble?"

"Indeed. Such is hindsight. But the fact that these two merchants would spend coin to deliver this message to me is worth knowing. I can trust these two."

"Mm. And yet the difference between reading and not reading the letters was the difference between heaven and hell."

"It's no joke. You've the right of it, no question. A single letter can determine your fate. A merchant without information might as well be heading out onto a battlefield with a blindfold."

"I don't know about your eyes, but you surely cover your shame often enough."

Lawrence was about to put the letters back into the envelopes when he heard this and froze, muttering an oath.

"Hmph. Even teasing you does not dispel my drowsiness." Holo yawned and hopped off the desk, walking over to the bed. Lawrence watched her bitterly. She turned to him.

"Oh, yes — we can go to the festival now, yes?" she asked as she picked up the robe that had been discarded on the bed, her eyes twinkling so brightly they were nearly audible. Seeing her thus, Lawrence wanted to take her out, but he had other business to attend to first.

"Sorry, not ye —"

Lawrence was cut off midsentence. Holo clutched her robe tightly, seemingly on the verge of tears.

"Even if you're joking, please — stop that, I beg you," he said.

"Ah-hah, so you *are* weak against this sort of thing. I'll remember that," said Holo, abandoning the act. Lawrence found he had nothing to refute her with.

Having had yet another weakness exposed, he turned back to the desk, defeated.

"Mm. But — can I not go into the town myself?"

"You'll go whether or not I give you permission."

"Hm, I suppose that's true…"

Lawrence returned the letters to their envelopes and turned to Holo once again; she held onto her robe, looking awkward.

At first he sighed inwardly — was she really playing this game again so soon? — but then he realized that without any money, she would be able to do little else than stare at the stalls, which to Holo was akin to a living death.

In other words, she needed marching money, but she couldn't bring herself to ask for it.

"I don't have any small change right now, so...don't spend it all in once place."

He stood and produced a silver *irehd* from the coin purse at his waist, then walked over to Holo, and handed it to her.

The coin bore the image of the seventh ruler of Kumersun.

"It's not as valuable as a *trenni* piece, so you shouldn't get the evil eye if you try to buy some bread with it. They'll make change without a fuss."

"Mm...," replied Holo indistinctly even as she took the coin. Lawrence instantly wondered if what she wanted was more money.

But if he betrayed this suspicion, she would really have him cornered.

Lawrence forced himself to maintain a neutral expression. "What's wrong?"

"Hm? Oh..."

One had to be careful when she was being so meek.

Lawrence's head shifted into negotiation mode.

"I was...I was just thinking that it would be a bit of a waste to go alone," Holo said.

And just like that, his mind spun fruitlessly.

"What business have you remaining? If you'll take me along, I'll return the silver piece," she said.

"Oh, uh, I was—I was just meeting with someone."

"Well, I'm going to wander about anyway. If you don't want me near, I'll keep my distance. Take me along, won't you?"

She wasn't being especially fawning or wheedling—she simply wanted to come along, it seemed.

If she'd cocked her head and said something like "Oh, do *please* take me with you!" he would have suspected her of putting on an act.

But her request was entirely normal.

If it really was an act, Lawrence felt like he wouldn't mind falling for it.

And in case it *wasn't* an act, Holo would surely be hurt by his suspicion.

"I'm really sorry—can you let me go alone today? I've got to meet with someone, and then I expect we'll be going elsewhere, so I can be introduced to someone else. If you came along, you'd have to wait outside nearly the whole time."

"Mm…"

"I should be able to finish up all my business today, and then starting tomorrow, we can take our time and enjoy the festival. So can you manage on your own for one more day?"

He talked with the same tone he would use on a girl of ten, but Holo—standing there beside the bed—looked roughly that vulnerable.

Lawrence understood how she felt.

It was precisely because he was not overfond of going to the winter festival alone that he came to Kumersun only in the summer.

Once the crowds became so thick that one could not help bumping into people, the loneliness became that much keener.

Going to a party at one of the trading firms and then returning alone to a lonely inn was similarly desolate.

Lawrence dearly wanted to bring Holo along with him, but this particular errand made that impossible.

He was going to be introduced to Gi Batos, thus making contact with the town chronicler that Batos evidently knew. One of the head masters of a trading firm Lawrence had visited also knew of the chronicler. Lawrence had taken the opportunity to find out more while he picked up his letters. As he suspected, the chronicler collected not only information on Ploania, but also wrote down pagan tales from farther north.

If the tales of Yoitsu were to come up, it could go badly if Holo was there to hear them. Since Lawrence knew one such tale — wherein Yoitsu had been destroyed by a bear spirit — he had trouble imagining that he would hear that Yoitsu was now prospering.

Hiding the fact forever would be difficult, but Lawrence thought he should at least try to reveal the truth to her at a suitable time. It was a delicate issue.

A moment of silence passed between him and Holo.

"Mm. Well, I do not wish to get in your way. I can't have you slapping my hand away again," she said, seeming even sadder — which was probably an act.

Nonetheless, the fact that Lawrence had slapped Holo back in Ruvinheigen still gnawed at him. The clever wisewolf in front of him knew this and was taking a bit of revenge for his refusal to give in to her request.

"I'll buy you a souvenir. Just abide one more day."

"So I'm to be bought off again, am I?" she said accusingly, but her swishing tail showed her anticipation.

"Shall I sweet-talk you instead?"

"Hmph. Your words are far from sweet; they're practically inedible. I shall pass."

It was a nasty thing to say, but Holo was smiling; her mood seemed to have improved. Lawrence waved a meek hand to indicate his defeat.

"I suppose I shall just wander about on my own."

"I'm sorry," said Lawrence, whereupon Holo spoke again as if she just remembered something.

"Oh, that's right. If when you return there are two people in the room, would you mind staying out for a while?"

For a moment, Lawrence did not understand what she was getting at, but he finally realized she was suggesting she might pick up a man while she was out.

58

Given her particular charms, Lawrence thought it could certainly happen.

But Lawrence had no idea what sort of expression he should assume in response to the statement.

Should he be angry? Should he laugh? By the time he concluded that ignoring her was the best course, Holo grinned at him with genuine delight.

"Seeing your adorable face will be quite enough to tide me over for the day," she said.

Lawrence found he could only sigh at her teasing.

Holo could be an infuriating wolf.

"I'd rather be in your arms than not, still," she said airily. "Do not worry."

Lawrence had no words.

She could be an *incredibly* infuriating wolf.

Lawrence opened the door to the trading company. It was afternoon, and the company indeed much more crowded than it had been earlier.

The building was filled with both town merchants based in Kumersun and traveling traders who operated in the area. The company was open but doing no real business since nearly everyone was there to enjoy the festival; the room overflowed with drinking and merriment.

Batos — the man acting as the intermediary between Lawrence and the chronicler — was evidently not as much of a drunkard as Mark has insinuated and had been out of the building on business when Lawrence came in the morning.

Lawrence asked after him with the chief of the trading company; Batos had still not returned, it seemed. Since he was meeting someone, Lawrence could not very well drink, and he mused on how to pass the time.

There were several other merchants in similar circumstances, but they had been seduced by the festive atmosphere and were absorbed in a card game, so Lawrence couldn't very well try to engage them in conversation.

There was nothing for it but to strike up some idle chatter with the trading house chief, who drank but likewise could not let himself get drunk. During their conversation, the doors opened and a single figure entered the trading house.

Lawrence and the chief were situated directly across from the entrance, so Lawrence could immediately see who came into the building. It was Amati, looking more like the young son of a nobleman than any merchant.

"Mr. Lawrence," said Amati after briefly greeting the men drinking by the door.

"Good afternoon. And thank you for your assistance with the inn."

"Not at all. I should be thanking you for ordering so much fish for dinner."

"My finicky companion praised it to the heavens. Said that you had an excellent eye for fish."

Lawrence felt this was a more effective compliment than saying he himself had enjoyed the food. He was correct.

Amati's face lit up like an excited boy's.

"Ha-ha, I'm delighted to hear it! If she has any other requests, I'll be buying some truly excellent fish tomorrow."

"She seemed to have a special love for the carp."

"I see...very well, then. I'll go find more that she'll enjoy."

Lawrence chuckled internally; at no point had Amati asked what *he* thought of the fish, but Amati no doubt had not even noticed this.

"Oh, incidentally, Mr. Lawrence — have you any plans at the moment?"

"I am killing time before I meet with Mr. Batos."

"I see..."

"Why do you ask?"

Amati's expression clouded over as he fumbled for words, but he resolutely overcame this in a manner befitting a merchant used to battling the fish markets day in and day out. "Er, yes, actually I was thinking perhaps I could show you and your companion around the town. Our meeting on the road was the will of God, surely, and I don't doubt I could learn much from talking with a traveling merchant such as yourself."

Amati sounded quite modest, but Lawrence knew that the boy had his sights set on Holo. If Amati had a tail, Lawrence was sure that it would be swishing back and forth excitedly.

Lawrence had an idea.

"I surely appreciate the invitation, and my companion Holo has been wanting to get a look at the town, but I don't think..."

Amati's expression changed. "If it's all right with you, I would be happy to show just Miss Holo around! In truth, I've finished my work for the day and am quite free."

"Oh, I couldn't possibly..."

Lawrence wasn't sure whether or not his feigned surprise was convincing, but Amati did not seem able to read Lawrence's expressions quite *that* well.

Amati, after all, was thinking only of Holo.

"Not at all. If left to my own devices, I fear I'll simply drink all my profits away. To be blunt, this works out nicely for me. I would be happy to escort her."

"I see. Well, she is not so well behaved as to stay in the inn simply because I told her to — she may not be there at all."

"Ha-ha! As it happens, I need to go by the inn and discuss a purchase with them, so I'll inquire after her while I am there, and if she is there, I'll invite her out."

"I'm so sorry to impose," said Lawrence.

"No, not at all. Please allow me to show you around town as well next time!"

Amati's skill with pleasantries marked him as a merchant through and through.

He must have been five or six years younger than Lawrence, but despite his callow appearance, he was no doubt a canny trader.

Though Amati's attention had been quite diverted by Holo, he remained thoroughly poised.

Lawrence was just musing on how he would have to be careful not to let his guard down around the boy when the trading company's door opened once again.

Amati looked toward the door at the same time as Lawrence. "Looks like I had good timing," said Amati, and Lawrence soon understood why.

As the saying goes, his party had arrived.

"Well then, Mr. Lawrence — I'll take my leave."

"Ah, yes. Thank you, again."

Whether he had no further business in the trading house or his head was so full of visions of Holo that he forgot why he'd come, Amati left the building.

Though Lawrence left her with some silver, he thought Holo was still probably lounging about in bed at the inn.

Given Amati's state, he'd be a perfect mark for Holo, who would have no trouble getting him to buy her whatever she wanted.

For a moment, Lawrence almost felt sorry for the poor boy, but he knew Amati would be all too happy to undo the strings on his coin purse for Holo.

Nothing would make Lawrence happier than Holo's mood being lifted on someone else's coin.

If only he could be so clever when dealing directly with Holo, he thought.

She did not just pull his leg — she swept it clean out from under him.

As Lawrence wondered if Holo's wit exceeded his own by as much as her age did, the man who entered the trading house just as Amati left scanned the room and then began to walk toward Lawrence.

Mark's apprentice had apparently run about the town to inform Batos of Lawrence's request, which was undoubtedly why Batos now approached him.

Lawrence greeted the man with a glance, flashing his merchant's smile.

"Kraft Lawrence, I presume? I am Gi Batos."

The hand that Batos extended in greeting was hard and rough, like a veteran soldier's.

Listening to Mark tell it, Batos was the sort of man who preferred drinking his profits away to actually making any, but upon meeting the man in person, Lawrence got precisely the opposite feeling.

As he walked down the street, Batos had a stocky stability about him that brought to mind a stout coffin, and his face had a tough, leathery quality (from years of exposure to wind and sand) out of which grew a spiky beard that was almost sea urchin–like. When Lawrence shook Batos's right hand in greeting, it felt nothing like the hand of an easygoing merchant who passed the days carrying nothing heavier than his cart horse's reins; it was rough and strong enough, telling that this was a man who did heavy lifting year-round.

Yet despite Batos's appearance, he was neither stubborn nor ill-mannered; the words he spoke had a priestly serenity to them.

"I daresay merchants who travel across many provinces, like yourself, Mr. Lawrence, are more numerous these days. Traveling to and fro between the same places, selling the same things as I do, gets quite boring."

"Ah, but the town peddlers and craftsmen would surely be angry if they heard you say so."

"Ha-ha-ha! Right you are. There are plenty of men who've spent fifty years selling naught but leather rope. No doubt I'd get an earful if I claimed to be tired of it," Batos said with a laugh.

He told of how he was a trader of precious metals from the mines of Hyoram and that he'd spent nigh thirty years going back and forth between those rugged mountains and the town of Kumersun.

Any man who could carry those heavy loads through the mountains of Hyoram — where the wind was strong and the trees were few — was a man to be reckoned with.

"Still, I must say you're a curious fellow, Mr. Lawrence."

"Oh?"

"I refer to your search for a chronicler to learn the ancient tales of the northlands. Or has it something to do with a business prospect?"

"Oh no, nothing like that. It's just something of a whim, I suppose."

"Ha-ha-ha! You've got good taste for one so young. I've only recently become interested in the old tales. Originally I intended to make a business of it, but I'm afraid they've quite become my master rather than the other way around!"

Lawrence couldn't quite imagine what Batos meant by making a business of the old tales, but the man's talk was intriguing, so he kept his mouth shut and listened.

"It came to me after so many years of going back and forth between the same places. The world I knew was very small, you see. But even there, people had been coming and going for hundreds of years, and I knew nothing about those times at all."

Lawrence had an inkling of what Batos meant.

The more he traveled around, the more the world seemed to spread out before him infinitely.

If that was the breadth of the world, in a sense, then what Batos felt was the world's depth.

"I'm old, you see, and I've not the vigor to go journeying afar. Neither can I travel back in time. So even if it's only by stories, I came to want to visit the places I've never been able to see in person and to travel back to those ages that God in his capriciousness has prevented me from experiencing. When I was a young man with nothing on my mind but profit, such things would never have occurred to me, but now I often wonder if I'd had the chance to consider them, my life would have turned out quite differently. So I must admit I'm a bit envious of you, Mr. Lawrence. Hah, I must sound quite ancient." Batos laughed at his own folly, but his words left a deep impression on Lawrence.

It was true that the old tales and legends allowed one to know of things that were impossible to experience directly.

He felt a new weight behind the words Holo had said to him not so very many days after they had first met.

"The worlds we live in, you and I, are very different."

For the greater part of the time Holo had lived, the people from her own era had been long since dead, the era itself lost to time.

And Holo was not human, but wolf.

Thinking on it, Lawrence saw that Holo's very existence began to seem special in more ways than one.

What had she seen and heard? Where had she traveled?

He began to want to ask her about her travels — perhaps when he returned to the inn.

"But when the Church looks at the old tales and legends, all they see are superstitions and pagan stories. Where the Church's eye falls, tales become hard to collect. Hyoram is a mountainous region and had many fascinating stories, but the Church was there, too. Kumersun is quite nice in that regard."

Ploania was a country where both pagans and the Church existed side by side, but it was precisely because of that coexistence that the Church was much stricter in those towns and regions where it held power.

Pagan towns that resisted Church control had to be constantly prepared for battle. Kumersun was unique in Ploania for its peaceful avoidance of those problems.

Even in Kumersun, it was not the case that there was a complete lack of conflict.

Lawrence and Batos headed to the north district of Kumersun in order to meet with the chronicler.

The town had been built with expansion in mind, so the city walls were constructed of wood that could be easily disassembled and the streets and buildings were spacious.

Yet even within this town, there existed a high stone wall.

The wall encircled the district housing those who had fled to Ploania because of Church persecution.

The very fact that the district was walled off with stone proved that the people of the town considered the presence of the persecuted a burden. While they were not considered criminals in Kumersun, in Ruvinheigen—for example—they would have been beheaded as a matter of course.

Upon reflection, Lawrence changed his mind.

The wall did not exist simply to isolate these people; it was probably necessary for their protection.

"Is that...sulfur?" Lawrence asked.

"Aha, so you've handled medicinal stones as well, have you?"

Hyoram boasted a variety of very productive mines, and while Batos may have been used to the distinctive odors of the region, Lawrence couldn't help but make a face.

The smell reached his nose as soon as they passed through the door in the stone wall, and he immediately knew what sort of people lived here.

The Church's greatest enemy — alchemists.

"No, I've knowledge of it is all."

"Knowledge is a merchant's greatest weapon. You're good at your job."

"...It's kind of you to say so."

The area within the walls was several steps lower than the outside ground.

The spaces between the buildings in the district were narrow, and although they called to mind alleys Lawrence had seen in other towns, there were some strange differences.

For one, many of the alleys they walked in were scattered with bird feathers.

"One can't always smell the poison wind. People keep small birds — and if the bird suddenly dies, they know to be careful."

Lawrence knew of the practice as it was used in mines, but having come to a place where it was actually employed sent a shiver up his spine.

The phrase *poison wind* was certainly descriptive, but for Lawrence's part, he felt the Church's phrase — *the hand of death* — to be more apt. Apparently it came from the fact that no sooner did one notice a strangely cold wind than one was paralyzed, unable to move.

Lawrence wondered if the cats that he saw here and there as they walked down the street were kept for the same purpose as the birds or if they instead gathered to prey on those birds.

In either case, it was eerie.

"Mr. Batos —"

It had been some time since Lawrence had found walking in silence to be so difficult.

The street was dim and strange, the silence punctuated by the meowing of cats and the flutter of birds; mysterious metallic sounds rang out occasionally, and the smell of sulfur was constant. Lawrence couldn't help raising his voice.

"How many alchemists are in this district, would you say?"

"Hmm...counting apprentices perhaps twenty, give or take. But in any case, accidents are common, so it is hard to know for sure."

In other words, there were a lot of fatalities.

Regretting having asked the question, Lawrence shifted to more mercantile concerns.

"Do you find that trading with alchemists makes good business? I would think it would bring significant danger."

"Mm...," said Batos slowly, stepping around a barrel that had held some green substance that Lawrence didn't want to look at too long. "There's a lot of profit to be had in trading with alchemists that have nobility backing them up. They buy a lot of iron, lead, quicksilver, and tin—to say nothing of copper, silver, and gold."

They were all quite normal commodities; Lawrence was surprised.

He had been expecting something much weirder—five-legged frogs, perhaps.

"Ha-ha-ha, are you surprised? Even here in the north, there are people who think alchemists are basically sorcerers. In truth, they're not so very different from metalsmiths. They heat metals or melt them down with acids. Of course..."

They turned right at a narrow intersection.

"...In reality, there *are* some who research sorcery." Batos looked behind them and then twisted his lip in a feral grin.

Lawrence faltered and stopped walking for a moment, at which Batos immediately smiled, apologetic.

"But I've only heard rumors of them, and I don't believe any of the alchemists in this district have met any such people. And incidentally, everyone living in this area is basically a good person."

This was the first time Lawrence had heard alchemists — who practiced their arts without any fear of God — described as "good people."

Whenever the subject came up, alchemists were spoken of in fearful, incurious tones, as though they had committed some unspeakable corruption.

"They're my bread and butter, after all, so I can't very well accuse them of being bad people now, can I?"

A slightly relieved Lawrence smiled at Batos's very merchant-like statement.

Shortly thereafter, Batos stopped before the door of one of the buildings.

The street received no sunlight and was riddled with holes and dark puddles of water.

The stone wall facing the alley had a wooden window that was cracked open, and the entire two-story building seemed to lean to one side.

It could have been a building from any slum in the world, but there was one important difference.

The area was completely silent; no peals of childish laughter sounded.

"Come now, you needn't be so nervous. They really are fine people here."

No matter how many times Batos tried to reassure him, Lawrence could only give an uncertain smile in return.

It was impossible for him not to be nervous — this was, after all, a place where people lived who had been branded criminals of the most serious sort by an authority that brooked no opposition.

"Excuse us — is anybody home?" Batos called out casually, knocking upon the door without any such fear.

The ancient door seemed like it had gone years without being opened.

Lawrence could hear a cat's quiet meow from somewhere.

A monk accused of heresy, chased out of a monastery — what kind of person would that be?

A shriveled old frog of a man appeared briefly in Lawrence's mind, clad in a tattered robe.

This was no world for a traveling merchant.

The door slowly opened.

"Well, if it isn't Mr. Batos!"

The moment was so anticlimactic that Lawrence very nearly collapsed.

"It's been a while. You seem well!"

"I could say the same of you! Spending all your time in the mountains of Hyoram. God must favor you indeed."

It was a tall, blue-eyed woman who had opened the thin wooden door. She seemed a few years older than Lawrence, but the fashionable robe draped comfortably around her body gave her a nonetheless fascinating aura.

Her speech was lively and pleasant — she was indisputably beautiful.

But in that instant, Lawrence thought of that which all alchemists sought — the power of immortality.

Witch.

The word appeared in his mind just as the woman looked at him.

"You're quite a handsome man, but you think me a witch — I can see it in your eyes."

The woman had seen right through him; Batos spoke quickly to smooth things over.

"In that case, perhaps that's how I should introduce you?"

"Don't be absurd — this place is already quite tedious enough. And in any case, is any witch as pretty as I am?"

"I hear many women are exposed as witches *because* of their beauty."

"You never change, Mr. Batos. No doubt you've hideaways all over Hyoram."

Lawrence had no idea what was going on, so he abandoned his attempts to grasp the situation and concentrated instead on calming himself.

He took one and a half deep breaths.

Then he straightened himself and became Lawrence the traveling merchant.

"So, m'dear. It's not me that has business with you today, but Lawrence here."

Batos seemed to have noticed Lawrence regain his composure; at his well-timed statement, Lawrence took a step forward, put on his best merchant's smile, and greeted the woman.

"Please excuse my rudeness. I am Kraft Lawrence, a traveling merchant. I've come to call upon one Dian Rubens. Might he be in the house?"

Lawrence rarely spoke so formally.

The woman stood with her hand on the door, silent for a moment, before smiling, amused. "What, did Batos not tell you?"

"Oh —" Batos lightly smacked his head with his hand as if to punish his own carelessness, and then he looked to Lawrence apologetically. "Mr. Lawrence, this is *Miss* Dian Rubens."

"Dian Rubens at your service. It's quite a masculine name, is it not? Please call me Diana," said the woman, her manner suddenly very elegant as she smiled. It was enough to make Lawrence feel that she must have been attached to a very well-to-do monastery indeed.

"Well, enough of that. Please, come in. I don't bite," said Diana with a mischievous smile as she gestured into the house.

The inside of Diana's home was not so very different from the outside — it called to mind the captain's quarters in a battered vessel that had been through a bad storm.

Wooden chests reinforced with iron bands were everywhere, piled in every corner of the room, their drawers left sloppily open, and there were sturdy, expensive-looking chairs mostly buried under clothes or books.

Also within the room were countless quill pens, as if some great bird had done its grooming in the room.

The only places in the room that seemed even marginally free from the chaos were the bookshelves and the large desk where Diana plied her trade.

"So, what might your business be?" asked Diana, pulling a chair out from under her desk, on which by some miracle of planning sunlight fell. She neither put hot water on nor gestured for her guests to sit down.

Tea or not just as Lawrence was wondering if she wouldn't do something about a place to sit, Batos took the liberty of removing items from one of the chairs turned into storage and gestured for Lawrence to sit.

Even the most arrogant nobleman would invite his guests to sit.

Lawrence felt no special malice behind Diana's eccentricity; it seemed part of her strange charm.

"First, I should apologize for my sudden intrusion," Lawrence said.

Diana smiled and nodded at the standard pleasantry.

Lawrence cleared his throat and continued, "Actually, Miss Rubens, I was —"

"Diana, please," she corrected him immediately, her expression serious.

Lawrence concealed his perturbation. "Excuse me," he said, and Diana's face resumed its soft smile.

"Yes, as I was saying, I have heard that you are quite knowledgeable about the old tales of the northlands. I was hoping you would share some of that knowledge with me."

"The north?"

"Yes."

Diana's countenance became thoughtful, and she looked at Batos. "And here I thought he'd want to talk business."

"You jest. Had he spoken of business you'd have had him out on his ear."

Diana laughed at Batos's words, but Lawrence got the sense that it was probably true.

"But you don't even know if I know the tale you seek."

"That might mean the tale I heard was made up from whole cloth," said Lawrence.

"Well then, it appears you will have to tell me this tale, and I shall do the listening."

Lawrence had to look away from Diana's kind smile as he cleared his throat again.

He was grateful Holo was not there.

"In that case, the story I wish to hear of concerns a village called Yoitsu."

"Ah, the one said to have been destroyed by the Moon-Hunting Bear."

Diana seemed to have immediately opened the drawers of her memory.

Given how quickly the subject of the town's destruction had come up, Lawrence again felt that leaving Holo behind was the right choice. It looked as though Yoitsu really had been destroyed.

His head hurt when he thought of how he would have to break this news to Holo.

As Lawrence thought this over, Diana stood slowly and approached the room's strangely well-ordered bookshelves, taking down a single volume from a neat row of large tomes.

"I seem to recall... Ah, here it is. The Moon-Hunting Bear, also known as *Irawa Weir Muheddhunde*, and Yoitsu, the village it destroyed. There are many stories of this bear. All quite old, though," said Diana smoothly as she scanned the pages. She had a callus on her index finger from writing, and it was swollen, making it seem quite possible that she had written all of these books.

How many pagan tales and superstitions were contained in those pages?

Something suddenly occurred to Lawrence. Batos had said he was thinking of making a business out of the old tales — no doubt he meant selling Diana's books to the Church.

With the stories in the books, the Church leaders would be able to instantly ascertain which heretical beliefs had penetrated which lands; they would do nearly anything for such information.

"It's not the bear I'm interested in, but the town."

"The town?"

"Yes. I've occasion to be searching it out. Is there anything in your tales that might reveal its location?"

Anyone would have been puzzled by Lawrence's question, which had nothing to do with the source for a commodity but rather the setting for an old legend.

Diana made an expression of surprise and then set the book on the table and began to think.

"Location, eh? Location, indeed..."

"Have you any ideas?" Lawrence asked again, at which Diana put one hand to her head as though suffering a headache and gestured for Lawrence to wait with the other.

As long as she was silent, it was easy to imagine this striking woman as the head of some solemn convent, but seeing her like this revealed an amusingly comical side to her personality.

Diana's eyes were screwed shut as she groaned with the effort of searching her memory, but then she suddenly looked up, happy as a maiden who had just succeeded in threading a needle.

"I have it! At the headwaters of the Roam River, which flows north of Ploania, there's a story like this in a town called Lenos," she said, suddenly and surprisingly as affable as she had been when speaking to Batos.

She seemed to forget herself when talking about old tales.

Diana cleared her throat, closed her eyes, and began to recite from an ancient legend.

"Long ago, a lone wolf called Holoh appeared in the village. Its great height was such that one had to look up to keep it in view. The villagers were certain that it was the punishment from the gods, but Holoh told of her journey from the deep forests of the east, explaining that she was bound for the southlands. She loved wine, and at times would take the form of a maiden and dance with the village girls. Her form was both fetching and youthful, though she kept her wolf tail. After frolicking with them for a time, she blessed their harvest and continued south. Since that time, bountiful harvests have continued, and we of the village remember her as Holoh of the Wheat Tail."

Lawrence was doubly surprised—both at Diana's smooth recitation and at the mention of Holo's name.

The name's pronunciation was slightly different, but it was unmistakably a story about Holo. Her blessing of the village's harvest supported that as did her maiden's form and retaining her lupine tail.

Yet this surprise paled in comparison to the content of Diana's tale.

The town of Lenos still existed at the headwaters of the Roam River. Using that as a reference point and knowing that there was a forest to the east Lawrence could draw a line southwest from Nyohhira and east from Lenos, which would put Yoitsu right at the intersection.

"Was that any use?"

"Yes, as it limits the area to the forest east of Lenos. It's a great help!"

"I'm so glad."

"I'll surely repay you as soon —"

Lawrence was cut off by a gesture from Diana. "As you can see, even if the Church pursues me for it, I love the old pagan tales — the ones that haven't been twisted out for consideration of Church beliefs. As you are indeed a traveling merchant, Mr. Lawrence, surely you have even one story you could share with me. If you'll do that, I'll require no further payment."

Those who composed histories for the Church did so to preserve the Church's authority. Historians retained by the nobility composed works praising their employers — this was simply the way of the world.

The Church's tale of Saint Ruvinheigen, namesake of the great Church city bearing the same name, was quite different from Holo's story of the man. The tale was deliberately rewritten to protect and extend Church authority.

Diana loved the old tales enough that she was willing to live in the slums of Kumersun, a town devoted to religious and economic freedom.

Lawrence wondered what terrible knowledge she must possess to have been chased from her cloister on charges of heresy, but now he saw that she simply loved the old tales enough to die for them.

"Understood," he said and began to tell his tale.

It was the tale of a place known for its bountiful wheat harvests.

And the tale of the wolf that ruled over them.

Eventually, once they had all gotten into some wine, they wound up talking of old tales and legends from all sorts of lands.

The sun was low in the sky when Lawrence finally remembered himself, and politely refusing Diana's invitation to stay, he left the house with Batos.

As he and Batos walked along the narrow street, neither could help laughing as they talked of the many stories they had shared.

It had been some time since Lawrence had enjoyed the tales of dragons and golden cities — he was well past the age when such stories were taken with anything but a large grain of salt.

Even after Lawrence had begun his merchant apprenticeship, he still longed to take up sword and shield and battle his way across the lands as a valiant knight-errant. As he traveled with his master across the countryside, the tales of fire-breathing dragons, birds so large their wings blotted out the sky, and sorcerers powerful enough to move mountains at will still set his heart secretly racing.

Of course, eventually he had dismissed such tales as pure fantasy.

It was meeting Holo that allowed Lawrence to enjoy them again.

Many of those old tales and legends were not fantasy at all, and even a humble traveling merchant might have adventures as great as any knight-errant.

That realization alone was enough to cause a warmth he had not felt in many years to spread throughout his heart.

In the midst of his giddiness, however, he remembered the events that happened during the attempt at smuggling gold into Ruvinheigen. He smiled at his folly.

He hadn't seen its form, but there was no doubt that a wolf not unlike Holo in those eerie woods near Ruvinheigen were the source of so much rumor. Lawrence, though, had been no strapping protagonist of a thrilling adventure. He was merely a helpless minor character caught up in the tale.

A merchant's life suited him much better, he felt.

Lawrence mused on this as they came to the broad street that led back to the inn. He took his leave from Batos there.

When Lawrence thanked Batos for acting as a go-between, Batos's reply was quick. "People tend to gossip if I go to Diana's place alone, so you were a fine excuse."

The lot back at the trading company were very fond of such talk.

"Ask me along anytime," Batos said. It was no mere pleasantry. He seemed to genuinely mean it. Lawrence, too, had enjoyed himself, so he nodded in the affirmative.

The sun was beginning to sink below the rooftops on the broad avenue, which was crowded with craftsmen returning home from a long day, traders winding up their negotiations, and farmers on their way home, having sold the produce and livestock they brought from their villages.

Lawrence headed south down the street into the central part of the town, where drunkards and children were added to the mix of the crowd.

Normally the number of town girls in the street tended to drop after sunset, but today they were plentiful, adding to the atmosphere of anticipation for the next day's festival. Here and there, circles of people gathered around fortune-tellers and the like, who did their business brazenly amid the crowds.

Lawrence cut his way through the throng and passed right by the inn along the street, heading straight for the market in the center of Kumersun.

Thanks to Diana, he had a general grasp of Yoitsu's location, and thus would not be heading for Nyohhira, but rather the town of Lenos.

Lenos was closer, and the road leading to it was better maintained. He also expected that once he was in Lenos he would be able to get more detailed information about the legends of Holo.

Thus it was that Lawrence found himself visiting Mark again. As Mark was gathering travel information for him, he needed to know about this change in destination.

"Hey there, lover boy."

As Lawrence approached Mark's shop, he saw Mark with a bottle of wine in one hand, looking merry indeed; the young apprentice he'd sent out to contact Batos earlier was now red faced and prone in the back of the shop.

It was Mark's wife, Adele, that attended to the closing of the shop, covering the piles of goods with a canopy against the evening dew.

As soon as she noticed Lawrence, Adele gave a slight nod and pointed to her husband with a chagrined smile.

"What's wrong?" said Mark. "Bah — here, have a drink."

"So about that information I asked you about this morning... Whoa, that's too much."

Mark didn't seem to hear Lawrence's protest at all as he poured wine from a ceramic wine bottle into a wooden cup.

His expression suggested that he would have nothing to say until Lawrence picked up the cup, which was now nearly overflowing with wine.

"Fine, fine." Exasperated, Lawrence took the cup and put it to his lips; it was good wine. He suddenly wanted some jerky to go with it.

"So, what was that? Have you changed your travel plans?"

"Indeed. There's a town, Lenos, at the headwaters of the Roam River. That's where I'm going."

79

"Well, that's quite a change indeed. And here I'd already collected quite a bit about the way to Nyohhira." If he had not been able to think clearly despite the wine, Mark would never have been a merchant.

"Apologies. Circumstances have changed a bit."

"Oh ho," said Mark with a smile as he gulped down wine as if it were water. He then regarded Lawrence with a look of amusement. "So it's true that things have gone bad with that companion of yours?"

There was a pause.

"What did you say?" Lawrence finally asked.

"Ha-ha-ha-ha. Word's gotten around, lover boy. Everyone knows you're holed up in a nice inn with a gorgeous nun. You've surely got no fear of God."

Kumersun was a large enough town, but it wasn't so large as Ruvinheigen—word spread quickly from one merchant to another until nearly all of them would have heard the news. The bonds between traders here were strong. If someone had seen Holo with Lawrence, word would get around.

If Mark knew about Holo, then everyone at the trading company would also know. He was glad he hadn't returned with Batos.

What he did not understand was why Mark said things had gone sour between Lawrence and Holo.

"We don't have the sort of relationship that makes for a good story over wine, but I don't see why you'd say things have gone bad with her."

"Heh-heh. The lover boy knows how to play dumb, that's for sure. But I can see the worry on your face."

"Well, there's no mistaking that she's a beauty. If things were to go poorly with us, it would be a shame."

Lawrence was surprised at his own ability to stay cool during the exchange — no doubt it came about because he was used to constant teasing from Holo.

Although truth be told, he felt he would have preferred for his business acumen to have gotten sharper rather than his patience.

Mark burped. "Why, just a moment ago, I heard that your companion was seen in the company of a young lad from our trade guild. Evidently they were getting on quite well."

"Ah, you mean Mr. Amati." Lawrence didn't feel comfortable calling the boy simply "Amati," and yet "Mr." suddenly seemed unnecessarily subservient as well.

"Oh, so you've given up already, then."

"You seem to be sadly mistaken. I simply had business today and was unable to accompany her, and Mr. Amati found himself with free time and wished to show us around town. These two events happened to coincide; that is all."

"Hmm..."

"You don't believe me?"

Lawrence had fully expected Mark to appear disappointed, so he found himself confused at Mark's look of genuine concern.

"I used to be a traveling merchant like you, so I'll give you some advice. Amati is more formidable than he seems."

"...What do you mean?"

"What I mean is, if you're careless, he'll snatch that pretty little companion of yours right out from under you. Men his age will do anything to gain the object of their obsession. And do you know how much fish Amati moves? It's a lot. And what's more, he was born in a pretty nice region of the south, but once he figured out that as the youngest child he'd never be allowed to make anything of himself, he ran away from home and came here to open his business. That was just three years ago. Quite a story, eh?"

It was hard to imagine the slight Amati doing all that, but Lawrence had seen for himself the boy's three cartloads of fresh fish.

81

What's more, Amati had been able to easily arrange a room at an inn facing a main avenue — albeit one to which he sold his fish. During a time when the town was overflowing with travelers coming and going, this was no mean feat.

A seed of fear began to take root in Lawrence's heart, but at the same time, he could not believe that Holo would transfer her affections so easily.

"No need to worry. My companion is not so fickle."

"Ha-ha-ha. You've a lot of faith. If I heard my Adele was out with Amati, I'd give up right on the spot."

"What's this of me and Amati?" said Adele, a truly frightful smile on her face. She had been behind Mark for some time as she cleaned up the shop in place of her husband.

Adele and Mark had fallen in love four years earlier when, as a traveling merchant, Mark had visited Kumersun. Their love story was quite famous in the town, and it was enough to make even a third-rate minstrel throw up his hands in disgust. She now possessed all the dignity of a wheat merchant's wife.

When Lawrence first met her, Adele had been quite frail, but now she was even more robust than her husband.

Two years previous she'd given birth to their first child — perhaps it was the strength of motherhood that she now had.

"Uh, what I was saying was that if I ever saw you out with Amati, why, you're so dear to me that the flames of my jealousy would burn my very flesh!"

"Burn away, dear. I'll just light a fire with the cinders you leave behind to make some tasty bread for Mr. Amati."

Adele was so caustic that all Mark could do in response was take another drink.

Perhaps women everywhere really are stronger.

"So then, Mr. Lawrence," said Adele. "Drinking in the company of this sot must make the wine taste poorly. We'll be closing up shop here, so why don't you come by the house and help yourself to some dinner? The baby may be a bit noisy, though."

Lawrence couldn't even begin to imagine how much mischief Mark's child would be capable of.

He was not especially good with children, but that wasn't why he declined the offer.

"I've still more business to attend to, unfortunately."

It was a lie, of course, but Adele nodded her regret without any trace of suspicion.

Mark, on the other hand, smiled as though having seen right through Lawrence. "Oh, indeed, you've unfinished business aplenty. And good luck to you."

Yes, Mark had seen the truth of it. Lawrence managed a weak smile.

"Ah, yes, so I'll keep your new destination in mind. I'll be keeping the shop open all during the festival, so I should be able to ask all about the route to Lenos."

"I appreciate it."

Lawrence finished off his remaining wine, thanked the couple again, and took his leave.

He noticed himself walking more quickly through the lively, bustling night and laughed at his own folly.

He'd actually claimed to have unfinished business — ridiculous!

But articulating the real reason made Lawrence hate himself, so admitting it to anyone else was out of the question.

Amati and Holo walking happily together — the image flashed briefly through his mind.

Despite his frustration, he noticed himself quickening his step more and more.

The boisterous clamor outside grew louder as the evening deepened. Lawrence was well into working out his upcoming travel plans with ink and pen borrowed from the inn when Holo finally returned.

Lawrence had hurried back to the inn only to find that Holo was still out, and although he'd had to swallow his disappointment, the time did give him a chance to calm himself, for which he was grateful.

Amati had taken his leave from her in front of the inn, Holo said, so she had come up to the room alone. Judging from the fox kit–skin muffler around her neck, Amati had been taken for quite a ride. There was no doubt in Lawrence's mind that she'd gotten him to buy her more than that.

His relief and happiness at seeing Holo's safe return was nothing compared to the headache that came with trying to figure out what would be an appropriate way to thank Amati.

"Ugh...it's too tight. Come...help me with this, won't you?"

However much she had eaten and drunk, Holo seemed incapable of taking off her own clothes.

Lawrence sighed and got out of his chair, walked over beside the bed, and undid the sash Holo struggled so valiantly against. He also removed the robe that was cinched up against her skirts.

"If you're going to lie down, take off your muffler and shawl. They'll wrinkle otherwise." Holo grunted vaguely in reply.

Lawrence managed to stop her from falling over onto the bed right then and there, and he helped her take off the muffler and rabbit skin shawl, as well as the triangular kerchief that she wore on her head.

Holo nodded off as she let Lawrence have his way with her clothing. She had probably parted ways with Amati in front of the inn because she was unable to keep herself together any longer.

Once Lawrence managed to get her out of the muffler, shawl, and kerchief, she immediately flopped down onto the bed.

Though he couldn't help smiling when he looked at the carefree wolf, Lawrence sighed when he glanced at the fox kit–skin muffler. He couldn't imagine buying such an item for resale, let alone as a gift.

"Hey, you — what *else* did you get him to buy you, eh?"

If Amati had gone this far, it seemed likely he'd bought her something still more costly.

Holo didn't even have the energy to lift her legs onto the bed, and her strange position remained unchanged as she took the long, slow breaths of the deeply asleep. The ears she was so proud of gave nary a twitch at Lawrence's question.

Realizing there was nothing else to do, Lawrence lifted her legs up onto the bed, and even then she did not so much as open her eyes.

He wondered if this utter defenselessness was due to trust or simply disdain.

He mulled it over for a while, but ultimately decided that such thoughts would only lead to disappointment, so he banished them from his head. Putting the muffler and shawl on the desk, he began to fold up her robe.

As soon as he did so, something fell out of the robe and hit the floor with a *clunk*.

He picked the object up; it was a beautiful metallic cube.

"Iron…? No."

It had sharp, carefully filed edges and a surface that was beautifully smooth even in the dim moonlight. Even if it *were* just metalwork, the cube would have been a valuable piece, but there was no telling how angry Holo would be if he woke her up just to ask about it.

He set the cube on the desk, deciding to ask about it the next day.

He put the robe over the back of the chair and folded the kerchief; then he rolled up the sash after smoothing out its wrinkles.

For a moment, he wondered why he was attending to these menial tasks — he was no manservant, after all — but one look at the sleeping Holo, snoring away artlessly on the bed there, was enough to dispel his indignation.

She had made no move to do it herself, so Lawrence walked over to the bed and drew the covers over her, chuckling.

He then returned to his desk and his travel plans.

If his circumstances didn't allow him to stay in the north while he searched for Yoitsu, he would simply have to change his business plan to accommodate some travel in the north. Whether or not he would actually follow those changes, there was no harm in making the plan.

Also, it had been some time since he'd really sat down with pen and paper and listed the towns, trade routes, commodities, and profit margins that made up the life of a traveling merchant.

He was filled with nostalgia when he remembered the times he had once burned the midnight oil to make such plans.

There was one large difference between then and now, though.

Were the plans being made for his own sake — or for someone else's?

Lawrence worked, pen in hand, listening to Holo's quiet snores, until the tallow candle burned itself out.

"Food, drink, the scarf, and this die."

"Anything else?"

"That was all. Well, that and enough sweet talk to fill a lifetime," said Holo lightly, chewing on the comb she used to groom her tail. Lawrence regarded her wearily.

He'd been relieved when she woke up without a hangover and had immediately interrogated her about the events of the previous night. Looking at the gifts she had received in the light of morning, Lawrence could tell they were of considerable value.

"So you ate and drank the night away, but then there's this muffler. I can't believe you'd go and accept such a thing..."

"It's fine fur, is it not? Though nothing compared with my tail."

"Did you make him buy this thing?"

"You think me so shameless? Why, he practically pressed it upon me. Rather fashionable of him, though, giving a muffler as a gift."

Lawrence looked at the fox skin piece, then at Holo. She continued, sounding pleased, "He's quite mad about me, you know."

"I'm sorry, did I ask for a joke? You can't just call it over and done when you receive a gift this valuable. Here I just thought to let someone else show you a good time, but now look at the debt I carry!"

Holo giggled. "So that was your plan all along, was it? I thought as much."

"I'm taking the consideration for this scarf out of your funds for the festival, just so you know."

Holo glared at him but turned away, doubly annoyed upon seeing that Lawrence glared right back at her.

"I trust you didn't show him your ears and tail at least?"

"You needn't worry. I am not quite *that* foolish."

Based on her state the previous night, Lawrence had not thought to worry about such a possibility, but now he wasn't so sure.

"I suppose you were asked what sort of relationship you have with me."

"What I would like to know is precisely why *you're* asking."

"If our stories do not match, people will begin to suspect things."

"Mm. Right you are. Yes, I was quite thoroughly questioned. I am a traveling nun and you saved me from being sold off by evil men is what I told him."

Aside from the part about Holo being a nun, that was more or less consistent with the truth.

"But once you saved me, I fell deeply into your debt, and as I cannot hope to repay it, I am gradually working it off by praying for your safety as we travel. Oh, alas and alack, woe is me! My voice was desperately sad as I told the tale. What do you think, eh? It has the ring of truth!"

Although it irked Lawrence that he seemed to be the villain of the story, it did seem convincing.

"As soon as I told the tale, he bought me the muffler," said the fake traveling nun with a frankly devilish smile.

"I suppose that will do. But what of this die? What made him buy you something like this?"

Lawrence had been unable to discern the color of the thing in the dim moonlight, but he could now tell that the cube of metal, so perfect it seemed the work of a master smith, had a distinctly yellow tint, like unpolished gold.

Lawrence had seen this kind of goldlike mineral before.

It was not the work of any human but entirely natural.

"Oh, that? The fortune-teller was using it. They say it's a die that can divine the future. It has a lovely shape, has it not? I can scarcely fathom how it was made. There's no doubt it'll sell for some fine coin."

"You fool. Do you actually think you can sell this?" said Lawrence, using the same tone she often rebuked him with. Holo's ears pricked up at the sudden harshness.

"This is no die. This is a mineral called pyrite. And no man made it."

His information was obviously unexpected. Holo regarded him dubiously, but Lawrence ignored this, plucking the yellowish crystalline cube off the desk and tossing it at Holo.

"I suppose the wisewolf that guarantees the harvest would know little of rocks. That die-shaped stone was mined just as you see it."

Holo smiled uncertainly, clearly disbelieving him, as she toyed with the pyrite.

"You should be able to tell that I'm not lying."

Holo murmured quietly and held the pyrite up between her fingers.

"It's not good for much, but it's often sold as a souvenir. And since it looks like gold, sometimes it's used by swindlers. Was anybody else buying it?"

"Oh, indeed. Many. The fortune-teller had great skill, enough to impress even me. He claimed that with dice like his, anyone could read the fates, so all that were gathered wanted the pyrite dice he was selling. He made up all manner of reasons why they were desirable."

"You mean the dice?"

"Indeed. Even the ones less perfect in shape than this he claimed would ward away sickness or evil."

Lawrence felt a certain professional respect for anyone who could invent such a lucrative business. Festivals and fairs often sparked strange fads.

The charged atmosphere made for great business, but pyrite — that was quite an angle, indeed.

"Amati bid down the price on that die, too."

This genuinely surprised Lawrence. "He bid it down?"

"The crowd had gotten quite enthusiastic. I'd not seen that sort of competition before — it was something to see, indeed. I expect I could sell the die quite dear now."

Lawrence thought of Batos, who traveled the Hyoram regions.

Did Batos know of this? If he had pyrite on hand or connections to gain it, there might be excellent business to be had here.

Lawrence had gotten that far in his train of thought when there was a knock at the door.

"Hm?" For a moment, he considered the possibility that Amati had spotted Holo's ears and tail, but then he decided that the perceptive Holo would have noticed if that were the case.

He looked from the door to Holo and saw that she drew the bedclothes up over herself. Evidently the visitor at the door was not of the dangerous sort they had encountered in Pazzio.

Lawrence walked over to the door and opened it.

On the other side was Mark's young apprentice.

"I apologize for calling so early in the morning. I have a message from my master."

It was hardly "early in the morning," and Lawrence couldn't imagine what was so pressing that it would inspire Mark to send his apprentice on an errand just when the market would be opening.

He wondered if Mark had perhaps fallen gravely ill, but no — were that the case, the boy would not claim to have a message from his master.

Holo shifted underneath the blankets, popping her head out.

The boy noticed and glanced her way. Seeing a girl on a bed covered from the neck down in blankets was evidently more than he had bargained for. He turned away, red faced.

"So what was the message?"

"Oh, er, yes. He said you needed to know right away, so I ran over immediately. Actually —"

The shocking news had Lawrence running through the streets of Kumersun a moment later.

CHAPTER THREE

The town of Kumersun rose early.

Lawrence crossed the broad north-south avenue and headed west toward the trading company. Here and there on the way, he spotted many people erecting what looked like signposts.

Lawrence glanced at them as he ran with Mark's apprentice. They seemed to indeed be signposts of some kind, but he could not tell what was written on them. It was a script he had never seen before, and the signs were decorated with flowers, turnips, or bundles of hay.

Undoubtedly they were used in the Laddora festival, which began today, but Lawrence had no time to investigate.

The boy was fleet of foot and showed no signs of tiring, perhaps from being worked so hard day in and day out by Mark. Lawrence had a fair amount of confidence in his own stamina but was hard-pressed to keep up. It was just as he was running short of breath that they arrived at the trading company.

The normally forbidding, tightly closed doors of the company were thrown open. A handful of merchants stood at the entrance, wine cups already in hand despite the early hour.

Their attention had been directed into the building, but upon noticing Lawrence's arrival, they beckoned him in with gusto.

"Hey! It's the man himself! Haschmidt the Knight has arrived!"

Hearing the name Haschmidt, Lawrence now knew for a certainty that Mark's apprentice had been neither jesting nor lying.

There was a romantic tale from the country of Eleas, a passionate nation of seas and vineyards.

The protagonist was Hendt La Haschmidt, a knight of the royal court.

However, Lawrence was far from happy to be called a knight.

Haschmidt the Knight fought bravely for Ilesa, the princess he loved. He challenged Prince Philip the Third to a duel for the right to her hand and died a tragic death.

Lawrence ascended the stone steps, pushing through the jeering merchants into the trading company.

Their gazes pierced him, spearlike, as though he was a criminal about to be crucified.

There at the back of the room, at the counter behind which sat the master of the firm, was his Prince Philip the Third.

"I say again!" cried a reedy, boyish voice that echoed through the lobby.

It was Amati — not wearing the standard oiled-leather coat of the fishmonger, but rather an aristocratic formal robe. He looked every inch the young son of a nobleman.

He leveled his gaze directly at Lawrence as the entire assemblage of merchants held their breath.

Right then and there, Amati held up a dagger and a sheet of parchment and made his declaration.

"I will pay the debt that now weighs upon the slender shoulders of this traveling nun — and when this goddess of loveliness does regain her freedom, I swear by Saint Lambardos, who watches over this Rowen Trade Guild, that Holo the nun will have my undying love!"

A commotion arose in the hall, laughter mixing with cries of admiration to create a strangely feverish atmosphere.

Amati ignored the noise. He lowered his hands and spun the dagger around, gripping it by the blade and holding the hilt out to Lawrence.

"Miss Holo has told me of her misfortune and ill treatment. I thus propose to use my fortune and position as a free man to regain for her the feathers of freedom, and furthermore to wed her."

Lawrence instantly recalled Mark's words the previous day.

Men his age will do anything to gain the object of their obsession.

He regarded the hilt thrust at him with a bitter gaze and then looked at the parchment.

Amati was just far enough away that Lawrence could not make the writing out, but it surely reiterated what the boy had just said in more concrete terms. The red seal at the bottom left of the sheet was probably not wax, but blood.

In regions without a public witness, or when one needed a contract with far more weight than a public witness could provide, there was contract law. The party who put their blood seal upon the contract would give the knife they used to the opposite party and swear an oath in God's name.

If the first party failed to fulfill the contract, they would be bound to kill the opposing party with that knife or else turn it to their own throat.

As soon as Lawrence took the knife offered to him by Amati, the contract would be sealed.

Lawrence did not move. He'd had not the slightest inkling that Amati's infatuation would come to this.

"Mr. Lawrence." The words were as piercing as Amati's gaze.

Neither flimsy excuses nor disregard would sway the boy, Lawrence guessed.

Desperate to buy himself some time, he said, "It is true that Holo is indebted to me and that she prays for me as we travel to repay that debt, but she will not necessarily abandon our journeying once that debt is lifted."

"True. But I am confident she will for my sake."

A murmur ran through the crowd, which was impressed at Amati's audacity.

He didn't seem drunk, but he was the very image of Philip the Third.

"Also, while she may not be perfectly devout, Holo is a nun, which makes marriage —"

"If you are worried that I do not fully understand the situation, then your concern, sir, is misplaced. I am aware that Holo is unattached to any convent."

Lawrence snapped his mouth shut to avoid the expletive that came to mind.

There were two types of so-called traveling nuns. The first type were women in a church-sanctioned mendicant order that nonetheless lacked a fixed base of operations. The second type were totally self-styled, unattached to any Church organization.

Such self-proclaimed itinerant nuns made up the greater part of the group, and they referred to themselves as such simply for the convenience it afforded them while traveling. Since they were not officially attached to any Church organization, they were not disallowed from marriage the way true nuns are.

Amati knew Holo was a self-styled nun, so it was too late to arrange any sort of pretense with a convent now.

Amati continued speaking, his voice smooth and confident. "It is in truth not my desire to propose a contract to you thus, Mr. Lawrence. No doubt everyone here thinks me like Philip the Third from the tale of Haschmidt the Knight. However, according to Kumersun law, when a woman is indebted, her creditor is considered to be her guardian. Of course —"

Amati paused, clearing his throat, then continued, "If you will unconditionally assent to my proposal of marriage, there is no need for this contract."

This sort of rare competition over a woman made for the best drinking stories.

The assembled merchants spoke in low tones as they watched the developing drama.

Most experienced merchants would not take Lawrence and Holo's relationship at face value. It would have been the height of naiveté to think that an indebted nun was really paying off her obligation by praying for her creditor as they traveled. It was much more likely that she didn't want to be sold off by whoever held her debt or that she was traveling with him simply because she wanted to.

Amati certainly realized this and undoubtedly thought it was the former.

Freeing the poor, beautiful maiden from the bonds of debt was a moral imperative that justified this ridiculous display of gallantry, Amati must have felt.

And even if he didn't think this, Lawrence still came away looking like the villain.

"Mr. Lawrence, will you accept this contract dagger?"

The merchants looked on, grinning silently.

The traveling merchant was about to lose his fetching companion to the young fishmonger out of sheer inattentiveness.

It made for rare entertainment — and there was no acceptable way for Lawrence to escape.

His only option was to best Amati by being the nobler man.

In any case, he didn't believe that if Holo's debt were paid she would stop traveling with him just because Amati told her to.

"I am not so careless to agree to a contract I have not read," Lawrence said.

Amati nodded, withdrawing the knife and extending the contract to Lawrence.

Lawrence walked toward Amati, watched by everyone in the room, and took the parchment, scanning its contents quickly.

As he expected, what was written there was a more tortuously worded version of the declaration Amati had just made.

What Lawrence was most interested in was the amount that Amati proposed to pay.

What had Holo claimed her debt to be?

For Amati to be so brimming with confidence, it had to be a relatively small amount.

Finally, he found the amount in one of the lines of the contract.

For a moment, he doubted his eyes.

One thousand pieces of *trenni* silver.

Relief washed over him, bodily.

"I assume this contract is to your satisfaction?"

Lawrence checked again, making sure there were no obvious traps hidden in the contract's language. He also looked for any points he might turn to his own advantage.

But the contract language was stiff enough to leave no such room to trip up the first party.

Lawrence had no choice but to return Amati's contract.

"Understood," he said, handing the contract back to the boy and looking him in the eye.

Lawrence reached out to grasp the knife, and the contract was sealed.

Every merchant in the hall — and more importantly, the patron saint of the trade guild, Saint Lambardos — was witness to the dagger contract.

The merchants raised their voices in a cry, clinking their cups together, bringing an end to the entertainment.

Amid the din, the two men looked at each other and left the contract parchment and dagger with the firm's master.

"The terms of the contract extend until the end of the festival — sundown tomorrow, in other words. Will that do?"

Lawrence nodded. "Bring the thousand *trenni* in cash. I will not accept a partial payment or anything less than that."

Even if Amati was the sort of merchant that routinely hauled three wagonloads of fresh fish, there was no way he would be able to simply produce one thousand *trenni*. If he were that successful, Lawrence would know about it.

Of course, if it was stock whose worth amounted to a thousand *trenni*, that could easily be produced.

To put it in the ugliest manner possible, this agreement amounted to Amati buying Holo for a thousand pieces of silver. Assuming Amati had no intention of trying to resell her somewhere else, it was as though a thousand pieces of silver were simply moving from Amati's pocket to Lawrence's.

If that was the case, Amati would surely have problems paying for his next day's stock of fish. Even if by some wild chance Holo *did* accept his proposal of marriage, what awaited them was a difficult future. The minstrels might claim that coin could not buy love, but the opposite was also true.

"In that case, Mr. Lawrence, we'll meet again here tomorrow."

His face still betraying his heightened emotion, Amati strode out of the guild hall. No one said a word to him, and soon all eyes were on Lawrence.

If he did not say something here, all would think him a mere rube taken for a ride by the cleverer Amati.

Lawrence straightened his collar. "I don't expect my companion will follow him simply because her debt has been lifted."

A grand huzzah arose from the gathered merchants, immediately followed by cries of "Double for Lawrence, four times for Amati — who's betting?"

It was a salt merchant of Lawrence's acquaintance who offered his services as a bookmaker—he caught Lawrence's eye and grinned.

The fact that the odds for Lawrence were lower meant that the merchants in this hall thought Amati's chances of winning were worse. The sense of relief he'd felt at seeing the sum of one thousand *trenni* in the contract was not wild-eyed optimism. Common sense dictated that Amati had overextended himself.

The bets rolled in, the majority of them on Lawrence. The more money that was placed on his odds for victory, the more his confidence grew.

Though his blood had run cold momentarily when Amati had made his proposal of marriage, the odds of it happening in reality were low.

Not only were the numbers against Amati—Lawrence took solace in knowing there was another barrier he would have to surmount.

Amati could never marry Holo unless she gave her assent.

On this point, Lawrence had absolute confidence.

There was no way Amati could know that Holo was traveling with Lawrence to the northlands.

He had told Holo already that knowledge was a merchant's best friend and that an ignorant trader was like a soldier walking blindfolded onto a battlefield.

Amati's situation was a perfect example. Even if he did manage to run all over town and scrape together a thousand *trenni*, in all likelihood Holo would remain with Lawrence as they traveled north.

He mulled the subject over as he apologized to the master for the unavoidable commotion and then put the guild hall behind him.

It seemed prudent to leave before the merchants finished placing their bets and the attention returned to him. He did not want to be the appetizer for their drinking.

Once Lawrence made his way through the considerable crowd and out of the hall, he recognized a familiar face.

It was Batos, who had introduced him to Diana the chronicler.

"It seems you've gotten wrapped up in quite a to-do."

Lawrence grinned, embarrassed, at which Batos smiled sympathetically.

Batos then continued ominously, "However, I think the young Mr. Amati has hit on a way to raise the capital."

Lawrence's smile disappeared at Batos's unexpected statement. "Surely not."

"I can't say it's the most admirable method, of course."

He couldn't be doing anything like Lawrence did in Ruvinheigen.

Kumersun lacked the steep import tariffs of Ruvinheigen, and with no tariffs, there was no point in smuggling.

"It won't be long before the news is all over town, so I can't say too much. If I show too much support for you, it wouldn't be fair to poor Amati — after all, he screwed up his courage and made that impressive declaration. But I wanted to give you some warning."

"Why?"

Batos grinned boyishly. "Whatever the circumstances, it is a good thing to have a traveling companion. It's hard to watch one be taken from a fellow wandering merchant."

Lawrence felt the sincerity in the man's smile.

"You might do well to return to your inn and formulate a counterplan."

Lawrence bowed to Batos as though Batos was a business partner who had just agreed to very favorable terms on a very large deal, and then he hurried back to the inn.

Amati had found a way to secure the funds.

Lawrence had miscalculated, but there were still things between him and Holo that Batos knew nothing about.

He turned the situation over in his mind as he walked down the broad avenue, whose traffic was limited owing to the festival.

He was confident that there was no way Holo would be swayed by Amati.

When Lawrence had returned to the inn and explained the situation to Holo, her reaction was unexpectedly vague.

She had been surprised enough upon hearing the message that Mark's apprentice delivered, but now she seemed to find the grooming of her tail to be the weightier matter. She sat cross-legged, her tail curling around her lap as she tended to it.

"So did you accept this contract?"

"I did."

"Mm...," she said vaguely, looking back down at her tail. Holo was unimpressed; Lawrence felt sorry for Amati.

He looked out the wooden window, telling himself there was nothing to be worried about, when Holo spoke abruptly.

"Listen, you."

"What?"

"What will you do if the boy actually gives you the money?"

He knew if he answered by saying "What do you mean, what will I do?" she would be unamused.

When she asked him questions like this, Holo wanted to know the first thing that came to his mind.

Lawrence pretended to think about it for a moment and then purposely gave a less-than-ideal answer. "After I'd calculated the amount you've used, I'd give it to you."

Holo's ears moved up slowly and she narrowed her eyes. "Do not test me."

"It's a bit unfair that I'm the only one who's tested, eh?"

"Hmph." Holo sniffed, unamused, then looked back down at the tail she tended to.

Lawrence had purposefully avoided saying the first thing that came to mind.

He wanted to test whether she had noticed that fact.

"If Amati should fulfill his part of the contract, I will certainly fulfill mine," he said.

"Oh ho." Holo didn't look up, but Lawrence could tell she wasn't really looking at her tail, either.

"Of course, you've been free all along. You may act as you wish."

"Brimming with confidence, aren't you?" Holo straightened her legs and dangled them off the edge of the bed.

It looked as if she was getting ready to spring upon him like she so often did, and Lawrence flinched but regained his composure and answered.

"It's not confidence. I merely trust you."

That was one way to put it.

There were any number of ways to indicate the same idea, but this one seemed the most gallant.

Holo was speechless for a moment, but her quick wits divined this soon enough.

She smiled and then stood up suddenly.

"In truth, you're much more charming when you're nervous."

"Even I can tell how much I've matured."

"So it's more adult to simply pretend composure?"

"Isn't it?"

"Having room to boast because you've seen a gamble that's to your advantage just means you're a bit clever. It does not an adult make."

Hearing the sage words of the centuries-old wisewolf, Lawrence made a suspicious expression, as though he were the subject of a shady sales pitch.

"For example, when Amati proposed the contract to you, would it not have been more admirable to refuse it?"

Far from it, Lawrence was about to say, but Holo cut him off. "But you looked around and judged whether or not you would be embarrassed."

"Uh—"

"Consider if our positions had been reversed. For example, thus—"

Holo cleared her throat, put her right hand to her breast, and began to recite:

"I cannot consider entering into such a contract. I wish to stay always with Lawrence. It may be a bond of debt that binds us, but it is still a bond. No matter how many different threads may entwine us, I cannot bear to cut even a one. Even if it shames me, I cannot accept your contract—or some such statement. What do you think?"

It was like a scene from a stage play.

Holo's expression had been absolutely serious, and her words echoed in Lawrence's heart.

"If someone said something like that about me, I would be beside myself with joy, I daresay," said Holo.

That was undoubtedly a joke, but she had a point.

Lawrence was not willing to simply admit her correctness—doing so was tantamount to admitting he was a coward who had only accepted the contract in order to avoid embarrassment. And in any case, being so frank and open in front of so many people was all well and good, but it would have had consequences.

"Well, that might have been the manly thing to do, but whether or not it's the adult thing to do is another issue."

Holo folded her arms, looking aside and nodding minutely. "True. It might be both the action of a good male and a reckless, youthful thing to do. One might be happy to hear it, but it is still rather rich."

"You see?"

"Mm. Now that I think on it, the actions that make a good male and those that make a good adult may be mutually exclusive. A good male is like a child. A good adult has a measure of cowardice."

It was easy to imagine a stalwart knight drawing his sword in anger at Holo's light dismissal of the male sex.

Lawrence naturally felt obligated to strike back. "Well then, how would Holo the Wisewolf, who is both a good woman and a good adult, respond to such a proposal?"

Holo's smile remained.

Her arms still folded, she replied, "Why, I would smile and accept it, of course."

Her light, effortless smile as she so easily claimed to agree to the contract made Lawrence realize just how profound her confidence and ease was.

He would have had no such ideas.

It truly was Holo the Wisewolf that stood before him.

"Of course, upon accepting the contract, I would return to the inn and, saying nothing, draw near to you like so —," she continued, unfolding her arms and walking toward Lawrence, backing him up against the windowsill. She reached out to him. "Then I would look down…" Her ears and tail drooped, her shoulders slumped, and she looked positively miserable. If this was a trap, it would be impossible to see through.

Holo's snicker that came soon after was genuinely frightening.

"Still," she said lightly, "you're a good enough merchant. You entered the contract because you think you can win. No doubt you'll do some under-the-table deals just to make sure."

Holo looked back up, her tail and ears flicking playfully. She spun around and arrived smoothly at Lawrence's side.

He soon understood what she was getting at.

"'Take me to the festival,' is it?"

"Surely a fine merchant like yourself isn't shy of bribery to fulfill a contract, right?"

Lawrence's contract with Amati did not directly involve Holo, but the true issue was whether or not Amati's marriage proposal would succeed. To put it bluntly, one thousand pieces of silver might or might not find their way into Lawrence's pocket depending entirely on Holo's mood.

For his part, Lawrence could hardly afford *not* to bribe Holo, on whose judgment this all depended.

"Well, I've got to go gather information on Amati either way. I may as well bring you along."

"What you mean is you'll take me to the festival and gather information on the way."

"Fine, fine," Lawrence replied, sighing as Holo jabbed him in the ribs.

The first thing that needed to be investigated was Amati's assets.

Batos had said the boy was going to use some not altogether admirable methods to get the cash, which Lawrence guessed was probably true. He couldn't imagine that Amati could produce a thousand *trenni* out of nowhere.

But it would be trouble if Amati actually pulled it off, so Lawrence headed to Mark's stall to ask his cooperation.

As Mark kept his stall open for the duration of the fair, he had missed the commotion at the guild hall and so readily agreed to help. With rumors spreading like wildfire but so few merchants having actually seen Holo's face, Lawrence's bringing her along to the stall was quite effective.

If it meant Mark would get to see the developments from a front-row seat, Lawrence thought it was a small price to pay for whatever favors were required.

"And anyway, it won't be me that's running about the town," Mark added.

Lawrence felt bad for Mark's young apprentice, but his was a path every merchant had to travel—it was a complicated emotion.

"Still, is it all right to be running around with the beautiful maiden of the hour?"

"She wants to see the Laddora festival. And besides, if I locked her up in the inn, it really would look like I was keeping her bound by debt."

"So Sir Lawrence says, but what is the truth of it?" Mark asked Holo, smiling. Holo was dressed in her usual town-girl clothes with the fox skin muffler Amati had given her wrapped around her neck. She seemed to understand what Mark was getting at. "The truth is just that. I am bound by heavy chains of debt. Through them I can see no tomorrow, and from them I cannot escape. If you were to free me from them, I would happily coat myself in wheat flour working for you."

Mark's face immediately split as he erupted with raucous laughter. "Bwa-ha-ha! Oh, that poor Amati lad. Lawrence is the one bound by you, aye!"

Lawrence looked away, not deigning to respond. He could see clearly enough that going up against both Mark *and* Holo would lead only to frustration.

Perhaps as a reward for his daily good conduct, Lawrence's savior appeared. Mark's apprentice arrived, pushing his way through the crowds.

"I've checked it out," he said to Mark.

"Oh? Well done. What do you have?"

The apprentice greeted Lawrence and Holo as he delivered his report to Mark.

There was no question that what he wanted was not a reward from Lawrence or Mark, but a smile from Holo.

Understanding this, she graced him with her loveliest, most demure smile. Holo's undeniable mischief caused the poor boy to turn red all the way to his ears.

"So what have you learned?" Mark grinned at his apprentice, who flailed for a moment before answering. Knowing Mark, Lawrence was sure the poor lad had been teased for some time.

"Ah, yes. Er, according to the taxation records, he was taxed on two hundred *irehd*."

"Two hundred *irehd*, eh? So that'd make it . . . what, about eight hundred *trenni* that Amati has on hand that the city council is aware of."

With a few exceptions, every merchant with a certain amount of assets was subject to taxation. The amount was recorded in the tax ledger, and anyone with a reason to do so could examine the records. Mark had gone through his acquaintances to take a look at Amati's tax records.

But there was no guarantee that a merchant would report his assets to the city council accurately, so it was better to assume he had some amount hidden away. In any case, as a merchant, most of his worth would exist in credit with other sources.

But Amati wouldn't be able to easily produce a thousand silver pieces to buy Holo.

Which meant that if he truly planned to fulfill the contract, he would have to resort to either borrowing, gambling, or some other method of realizing short-term gains.

"Where's the town gambling hall?"

"Hey, just because we keep the Church in check doesn't mean it's a free-for-all. It's pretty much limited to cards, dice games, and rabbit chasing. There's also an upper limit on how much you can bet. He's not going to raise the money gambling."

Given the precision and detail with which he had answered the short question, it seemed Mark, too, was trying to work out how Amati could possibly raise the funds.

After all, Amati was essentially proposing to spend a thousand silver pieces on something he would never be able to resell, so any merchant would be curious as to the source of such wealth.

Lawrence was deep in thought, trying to decide what to investigate next, when Mark suddenly spoke.

"Oh, that's right. Apparently there's another bet on — about what's going to happen after the contract."

"*After* the contract?"

"Yes, if Amati wins the contract, who will be the victor *after* that."

Mark grinned provocatively; Lawrence turned away, his face betraying his irritation.

Holo had evidently taken an interest in the grain and flour laid up in Mark's shop, and she wandered about, listening to the apprentice's grand explanations.

She seemed to hear Mark and Lawrence and looked their way.

"But you've got the advantage as far as the odds go."

"Maybe I should demand the bookmaker give me a cut."

"Ha-ha-ha. So what are you actually going to do?"

Mark was obviously trying to get some information that would allow him to make some money on the wager, but he also seemed genuinely curious.

Lawrence only shrugged, not giving a proper answer to the question, but then Holo (who had evidently approached the two at some point during their conversation) spoke.

"Even if a question has a proper answer, sometimes one cannot simply give it away. For example, the mixing of your flour there."

"Erk —" Flustered, Mark shot his apprentice a sharp look, but the boy merely shook his head, as if to say, "I didn't tell her anything!" The mixing of the flour surely referred to its purity. Mixing in cheaper grades of flour with wheat flour to increase its volume was a standard merchant trick.

Even a merchant that dealt with flour day in and day out would probably have a hard time noticing small fluctuations in purity, but for Holo, whose very spirit resided within the wheat, it was simplicity itself.

She continued, "You want to ask what I'll do if he truly pays my debt, do you not?"

She gave the unfriendly smile that was her specialty.

Mark now shook his head frantically, much like his apprentice, as they looked to Lawrence with beseeching eyes.

"At this point, all we can do is observe our opponent's actions," said Lawrence.

"How treacherous."

Holo's sharp appraisal pierced Lawrence's heart.

"I'd be happier if you called it a hidden contest. He'll certainly have someone watching our moves as well, you know," Lawrence said.

Mark recovered his composure enough to differ. "I wonder about that. Amati ran away from home and came alone all the way to this town, achieving all his success independently. And there's his youth to consider. He's very self-confident. Not only does he not give much thought to the connections between merchants, he would probably consider tricks like that beneath him. He trusts only in his eye for good fish and his ability to sell them. That and the protection of the gods."

Amati sounded more like a knight than a merchant to Lawrence, who found himself envying the boy's ability to achieve such success on his own.

"That'd explain why he'd fall so hard for a charming girl who'd just arrived in town," Mark continued. "The townswomen are even more closely connected than the merchants. They seem to care only about reputation and are always watching each other. If one starts to stick out a little more, the others beat her down. I'm sure he finds it distasteful. Of course, not *all* women are like that, as I found out when I married my Adele."

As a traveling merchant, Lawrence well understood Mark's explanation. The town could certainly look that way from the outside.

Lawrence glanced sideways at Holo. He felt that yes, if he was in similar circumstances and saw a girl like Holo, he might well fall for her instantly — all the more so if he thought she was just an ordinary girl.

"Amati may well be as you say, but I will not hesitate to use any connection I need to. Treachery may be forbidden when knights duel, but there's no crying in a contest of merchants."

"I surely agree," said Mark. He looked at Holo.

Lawrence likewise looked at her again. Holo put her hands to her cheeks in a gesture of embarrassment, as though she had been waiting for the moment, and spoke.

"I wish just once someone would attack me from the *front*."

No doubt Mark was finally realizing, Lawrence mused, that there was no winning against Holo.

In the end, Lawrence decided to use Mark's connections to get more information on Amati. He made sure to mention to Mark the peddler Batos's hint regarding Amati's potential reserves of capital.

Lawrence trusted Holo, but there was no telling what she would do if he rested on his laurels in this contest. And there was always the possibility of being able to make some money in Amati's wake.

Holo and Lawrence couldn't very well hang around Mark's shop all day long, so after Lawrence asked Mark to help him with information, they put the stall behind them.

The town was becoming livelier and livelier, and the crowds did not diminish at all as they passed from the market to the plaza.

Midday approached, and people lined up in front of every stall alongside the road. Holo was not shy about lining up herself, clutching the money she'd relieved Lawrence of.

Lawrence watched her from afar, thinking it was just about time for the midday bell to ring, when he heard a low, lazy tone sound.

"A horn?"

The horn's sound made him think of shepherds, and for a moment, he remembered Norah and the danger they had faced together in Ruvinheigen. If the keen-eyed Holo saw through him, though, it would be trouble.

Lawrence chased the thought from his mind and tried to see where the sound came from just as Holo returned, bearing the fried bread she'd managed to successfully buy.

"Did I not just hear a shepherd's horn?" she asked.

"You did. I wasn't sure, but if you call it a shepherd's horn, then it must be so."

"It fairly overflows with the scent of food here. I cannot tell if there are sheep or not."

"There would be sheep aplenty in the marketplace, but there's no need to blow a horn in town."

"And no comely shepherdesses."

Lawrence had been expecting the jab, so he was relatively unaffected.

"Hmph," said Holo. "When you fail to react, it does rather feel like I am trying to win your affection."

"I'm just terribly delighted. *Scarily* so."

Holo happily bit into her bread with an audible crunch. Lawrence chuckled and looked out over the plaza again, realizing that the crowd seemed to be flowing in a particular direction. People were heading for the center of the city. Perhaps the horn had been the signal for the opening of the festival.

"Sounds like the festival has begun. Shall we go see?"

"'Twould be boring to do naught but eat."

Lawrence's smile was a bit forced as he started walking; Holo took his hand and followed.

They moved with the crowds, bearing north along the marketplace's edge, until eventually they began to hear cheers amid the sounds of drum and horn.

All manner of people were gathering—town girls dressed much like Holo, apprentice craftsmen (their faces black with soot after having snuck away from their work), itinerant priests with the customary three feathers pinned to their robes, and even lightly armored men who might have been knights or mercenaries.

The noise seemed to come from the intersection of the two main streets that quartered the town, but the crowds made it impossible to see. Holo craned her neck to try and catch a glimpse ahead, but even Lawrence couldn't see past the crowds, and he was much taller than Holo.

Lawrence remembered something, and taking Holo's hand, he ducked into an alleyway.

Once they were a few steps into the alley, things were much quieter, unlike the clamorous street. Here and there were beggars clothed in rags, dozing away as though to proclaim their disinterest in the festival, along with craftsmen who busily prepared the wares they would sell in their stalls, their workshops open to the alley.

Holo soon seemed to understand where they were heading and silently followed.

If the festival was being held in the main streets, they would be able to see the sights perfectly well from their room at the inn.

Holo and Lawrence walked easily down the uncrowded back

alleys, entering the inn from its rear door and climbing to the second floor.

It seemed that someone else had the same idea and was making a business out of it. As they arrived on the second floor, they noticed several of the doors along the hallway leading to their room had been left open and a bored-looking merchant sat on a chair in front of them, idly playing with a coin.

"We'll have to be thankful to Amati on this count anyway."

Upon entering their room and opening the window, they immediately had front-row seats.

To see everything that was happening at the large intersection, Holo and Lawrence had but to lean a bit out the window, and even without leaning, they had a perfectly acceptable view.

The musicians playing pipes and drums in the intersection were clad head to toe in ominous black robes that obscured even their sex.

Behind the group in black walked another strangely dressed troupe.

Some of the costumes consisted of sewn-together pieces of clothing large enough to cover any number of people. Such a costume had several people hidden underneath it and was topped with a mask where the head would be. Other performers wore robes that concealed what must have been one person riding on another's shoulders, their head popping out of the top of the garment. Some carried great swords made from thin pieces of wood; others had bows taller than they were. They brandished the weapons wildly to great cries from the crowd.

But just as Lawrence thought that was all there would be, there was a noticeably louder shout from the crowd, and a new set of instruments could be heard.

Holo gave a small cry of surprise, and Lawrence leaned his head out the window so as not to block her view.

The inn sat at the southeast corner of the intersection, and it seemed another group in strange costumes was emerging from the east.

Leading the group were people clad in black, but behind them followed another group whose dress was wholly different from those who currently occupied the intersection.

Some people had paint-blackened faces and wore cow horns upon their heads; others carried bird wings on their backs. Many were covered in animal skins of some sort, and it seemed likely that if Holo was to walk among them with her ears and tail exposed, no one would bat an eye. After that column passed, there arose a riotous cry and with it appeared a giant straw figure far bigger than a human. It was vaguely lupine in shape, four legged, and larger even than Holo's wolf form. The figure was supported on a wooden rack, which was carried by ten men or so.

Lawrence was about to say something about it to Holo, but he abandoned the notion when he saw the intense focus with which she watched the festival.

Animal costume after animal costume appeared in the intersection-cum-stage as the column continued along.

The black-painted marchers at the head of the procession now pointed at the signposts that had been erected here and there in the intersection, milling about as they did so.

Seeing this, Lawrence guessed that this was no mere costume parade. He thought there was some kind of tale being told — unfortunately, he was not sure. He was just thinking he would ask Mark about this later when he saw another procession arrive from the north.

These were normal folk, though some were dressed in tatters, some in noble robes, and some as knights and soldiers. The single commonality was the spoon that each one of them carried. Lawrence wondered why *spoons*, of all things, when the three groups collided in the intersection and began crying out in a language he had never heard. A slight ripple of nervousness ran through the assembled spectators as they watched the exchange; Lawrence, too, felt some trepidation.

Just as he was wondering what would happen next, the black-clad group all pointed in the same direction as one.

It was southwest that they pointed, and everyone's gaze soon turned that way.

Carts loaded with large barrels had evidently been prepared beforehand. Their stewards laughed loudly (if somewhat forcedly) and pushed the carts into the intersection.

The black-clad people began to play the instruments they held, the people in costumes began to sing, and the barrel carriers opened the barrels and began to sprinkle their liquid contents about.

As if that were some kind of signal, the onlookers now flooded into the intersection and began to dance.

The ring of dancers expanded rapidly. Many of the strangely dressed revelers had jumped out of the intersection and danced along the sides of the streets.

The merriment spread, and in no time at all, the entire boulevard was a huge ballroom. In the middle of the intersection, the participants of the original procession linked arms and began to dance in a circle. The festival was well and truly under way now; the singing and dancing would continue into the night.

It seemed that the opening of this festival — this *revel* — was complete.

Holo pulled her body — which heretofore had leaned well out of the window — back into the room.

"I'm going to go dance," she said, though it was not clear if she spoke to Lawrence or not.

Lawrence could count the number of times he'd danced like this on one hand. He tended to avoid festivals such as this one, and dancing alone was always a depressing affair.

Thus he hesitated for a moment, but he soon changed his mind after seeing Holo's outstretched hand.

Everyone would be drunk anyway — no one would notice if his dancing was a little clumsy.

And Holo's outstretched hand was worth ten thousand gold pieces.

"All right," said Lawrence, taking Holo's hand and preparing himself.

Holo laughed at his overserious resolve. "Just mind you don't tread on my feet," she said with a smile.

"...I will do my best."

The two exited the inn and plunged into the reveling crowds.

How many years had it been since he'd celebrated so much?

Lawrence had danced, drunk, and laughed so much he could not help but wonder.

This was also certainly the first time he had basked thus in the post-revel afterglow.

Normally, once the fun had passed, it was followed by a rush of terrible loneliness.

But as he helped Holo, unsteady on her feet from a surfeit of merriment and wine, up the inn stairs, the heat of the moment faded to a pleasant warmth. As long as Holo was with him, he felt, the celebration would continue.

The inn room's window had been left open, and the sounds of the continuing festival filtered though it. The night was young, and the merchants and craftsmen who had to work through the day were only now beginning to join in the festivities.

The festival seemed to have entered a new phase. As they

returned to the inn, Lawrence had looked back at the intersection to see it filled with people busily coming and going.

If Holo had had any strength remaining, she surely would have wanted to see. Unfortunately, she was exhausted.

After putting her to bed and setting her things in order (continuing his manservant duties from the previous day), Lawrence sighed.

It was not, however, an unhappy sigh. It came out as he looked at Holo's flushed cheeks as she lay sideways and innocent on the bed.

He felt a bit bad for Amati. He was no longer even remotely worried about having to fulfill the contract.

Far from it — in fact, he'd forgotten about it entirely until they had returned to the inn.

Once they came back, the innkeeper told Lawrence there was a message for him. It was from Mark; the message was "I've found how Amati plans to make the money — come to the shop as soon as you can."

The first thought that crossed Lawrence's mind was *I'll go tomorrow.* Normally such procrastination would never have occurred to him, and when he thought on it, it illustrated just how low of a priority it was for him.

What concerned him more than Mark's message was the letter that had come with it. It was sealed with a wax stamp and had "Diana" written in a lovely hand on the envelope. The letter had apparently been delivered by a stout man with a coffin-like build, which had to be Batos.

Lawrence had asked the chronicler to please let him know if she should happen to recall anything more about Yoitsu, which is what he expected the letter to be about. He considered opening it right then and there, but he decided that once he sat down and opened the envelope, he would be even less inclined to go visit Mark, so he decided against it.

Lawrence slipped the envelope back into his coat, and closing the window against the clamor still wafting in from the street, he headed out.

Just as he was about to open the door, he felt a gaze on his back, and looking behind him, he saw Holo forcing her sleep-heavy eyes open to look at him.

"I'm just going out for a bit."

"...Quite, and with a letter from a female tucked near your breast?" Her irritation did not seem to come from her struggle to stay awake.

"Aye, and she's a beauty, I might add. Does it bother you?"

"...Fool."

"She's a chronicler. Do you know what that is? She's the one telling me about Yoitsu. She's quite knowledgeable about the tales from the northlands. I haven't read the letter yet, but just talking to her yesterday gained us some excellent information. I even heard a story about you."

Holo rubbed her eyes like a cat washing its face, and then she sat up. "...A story? About me?"

"A town called Lenos has a story of you. Holoh of the Wheat Tail. That's you, is it not?"

"...I've no idea. But what do you mean by 'excellent information'?" With her homeland as the subject of conversation, Holo was now fully awake.

"Part of the tale included the direction from which you arrived in the town."

"I-in..." Holo's eyes widened and she froze, emotion writ large on her face. "In truth?"

"I've no reason to lie, do I? Evidently you arrived in Lenos from the forest east of it, so the mountains southwest of Nyohhira and east of Lenos are where we'll find Yoitsu."

Holo's hands gripped the bedclothes tightly, and she looked down upon hearing the unexpected news. Her wolf ears trembled as though each hair were overflowing with joy.

Hers was the relief of a girl who'd long ago lost her way but had finally found a familiar path.

Slowly and carefully she took a deep breath, which she then exhaled forcefully.

It was only her wisewolf's pride that kept her from bursting into tears right there on the spot.

"I'm surprised you didn't cry."

"…Fool." Her sneer proved how close to tears she had actually come.

"Knowing only that it was to the southwest of Nyohhira would have made the search difficult, but now it will be much narrower. I haven't opened the letter yet, but I'm sure it has additional information. It should be much easier to find our destination now."

Holo nodded and looked aside; then still holding the bedclothes, she looked back to Lawrence searchingly.

Her red-tinged amber eyes sparkled with a mixture of anticipation and doubt.

The white tip of her tail flicked to and fro uncertainly, and she looked so much the frail maiden that Lawrence couldn't help but smile weakly.

If he'd failed to understand what she was saying with that gaze, he would have no cause for complaint when she ripped his throat out.

Lawrence cleared his throat. "I daresay we'll be able to find it within a half year."

He could tell that the blood was once again flowing through her stone-still form.

"Mm!" said Holo happily with a nod.

"So the sender of this note is like a dove bearing good news. Go reflect on your misguided assumptions."

Holo's lips twisted in displeasure, but Lawrence could not fail to notice that it was an affectation.

"In any case, I'm now off to see Mark."

"With a letter tinged with a female's scent tucked near your breast?"

Lawrence couldn't help but laugh at Holo repeating her pointed question.

No doubt she wanted him to leave the letter.

She could not come right out and say as much, though, because it was too embarrassing to admit she was so nervous that she wanted him to leave a letter she could not even read.

Amused at the normally opaque Holo's transparent state of mind, Lawrence handed her the letter.

"You said the sender was a beauty?"

"Oh, indeed, and fairly wrapped in adulthood."

Holo raised a single eyebrow. She took the letter and then looked back to Lawrence, her eyes narrowed. "You're becoming a bit *too* adult and cunning." She grinned, revealing her fangs.

"Also, apparently Amati's found a way to raise the thousand silver pieces he needs. I'm off to ask about that."

"Oh, aye? Well, do try to come up with some way to prevent me being purchased away, hmm?"

Given their exchange thus far, Lawrence did not take Holo's words too seriously.

"If you want to read the letter, feel free to open it. If you *can* read, that is."

Holo sniffed and flopped over on the bed, letter in hand, her tail waving as if to say, "Well, run along now." She was like a dog carrying a bone back to its den.

He wouldn't dare to say as much, though, so he smiled wordlessly and, opening the door, left the room.

Just before he closed the door behind him, Lawrence looked back at Holo one last time, whose tail waved as though she had expected him to take one last look.

He chuckled and closed the door slowly so as not to make a sound.

"I must say, for someone asking a favor, you don't seem too worried."

"Apologies."

Lawrence had debated going straight to Mark's home but decided the man was probably still at his marketplace stall, which turned out to be correct.

Among the stands scattered here and there in the marketplace, people toasted each other's health in the moonlight, and even many of the guards responsible for watching over their masters' goods had succumbed to their desires and were drinking.

"Though I suppose I've time to spare aplenty during the festival," Mark admitted.

"Oh?"

"Oh, indeed. No one wants to lug heavy goods about while they take in the sights, do they? Especially something as bulky as wheat, which I sell before the festival begins and buy once it ends. Of course, the night festival is a different matter, though."

The night festival was held after the two-day festival finished, and it amounted to a great feast, Lawrence had heard. It was not as though he didn't understand the desire to use the festival as an excuse to drink and revel.

"And anyway, I've already turned a bit of a profit thanks to your information, so I suppose I'll let you off the hook this time." Mark's smiling face was every inch the pleased merchant.

Evidently he'd taken advantage of whatever it was Amati was up to.

"So you're on board, eh? What's his trick?"

"You're going to like this. I don't mean the trick is just clever — I mean it's like picking up gold off the street."

"I'm all ears," said Lawrence, sitting down in a conveniently close split-log chair.

Mark grinned at what this implied. "I hear tell the knight Haschmidt is quite a dancer. If he keeps making merry like this, he may have to take the thousand silver and lose the lovely maid."

"You're certainly welcome to bet your whole fortune on Amati — it makes not a whit of difference to me."

Mark blocked Lawrence's attack not with his shield, but his sword. "That Philip the Third has been saying some interesting things about you."

"Oh?"

"That you keep the poor girl in debt simply so you can take her wherever you please, that you treat her cruelly and feed her nothing but cold porridge — and so on."

Mark was obviously amused, as though it were a grand joke, but Lawrence could only listen and smile uncomfortably.

Amati was obviously spreading rumors about Lawrence as a way to justify his own actions. Lawrence's cheek twitched, more from the annoyance of this mosquito buzzing around his face than from the damage done to his reputation.

A traveling merchant was no sword-wielding mercenary — he couldn't simply foist debt off on any girl he wished, forcing her to travel with him. Even if a note of debt was written in a city where the merchant had some pull, it would be meaningless as soon as they were on the road.

Likewise, anyone used to long journeys would know there was

nothing surprising about the meager food one ate during travel. Any merchant who'd tried to maximize profit knew that there were times one went without food.

So Amati's slander of Lawrence would not be taken seriously. That was not the problem. What irked Lawrence was that Amati spread the notion that he and Lawrence were in the same ring, fighting over a woman.

Even if that didn't have a direct effect on Lawrence's business, it was hardly something to be happy about in regards to his standing as an independent trader.

Mark surely knew how irritating this would be, which explained his self-satisfied smirk. Lawrence sighed and waved his hand as if to end the discussion. "Anyway, what's this talk of profit?"

"Ah, yes. Once I'd heard that old Batos had figured it out, I put the pieces together."

So it was something to do with Batos's business.

"Precious gems, then?"

"Close, but no. You can hardly call it 'precious.'"

The commodities that ore merchants bought and sold as they traveled through mining country ran through his mind. Suddenly, Lawrence had it.

The mineral he'd talked about with Holo that looked like gold —

"Pyrite?"

"Oh, so you've already heard?"

Apparently that was the answer.

"No, I'd just thought it might make a good business myself. Because of the fortune-teller, right?"

"That's what they say. Though that fortune-teller's already left town."

"I see."

A sudden cheer grabbed Lawrence's attention; he looked to see a group of men in traveling clothes joyfully greeting some town merchants, embracing one another heartily at their evidently happy reunion.

"Yeah, the public story is that his fortune-telling was too good, so he was attracting the eye of a Church inquisitor, but that sounds pretty suspicious."

"Why suspicious?"

Mark took a sip of wine and removed a small burlap sack from the shelf behind him.

"First of all, if an inquisitor had actually come to town, it would be huge news. Secondly, there's just a little too much pyrite in circulation right now. My guess is he bought up somewhere else and left as soon as he'd sold all his stock. Also..."

Mark dumped the contents of the bag out onto the table. Some of the pyrite pieces had that beautiful die shape; others were as misshapen as flattened bread.

"I think he was trying to exaggerate the rarity of pyrite. How much do you think this is worth right now?"

In his hand, Mark held a die-shaped piece, which was generally considered the most precious form of pyrite. Standard market value was perhaps ten *irehd*, or one-quarter of a *trenni* piece.

But Holo had said the pyrite piece Amati gave her had been bought at an auction, so Lawrence made a bolder guess.

"One hundred *irehd*."

"Try two hundred seventy."

"Im—"

—*possible*, he was about to say, but he swallowed the word, cursing himself for not buying up stock immediately after Holo told him of the pyrite.

"To men like us, that'd be a ridiculous price even for a precious gem. But when the market opens tomorrow, it's going to rise even higher. Right now every woman in town is scheming to buy. Fortune-telling and secret beauty potions will always be in demand."

"But still — two hundred seventy? For *this*?"

"It doesn't even have to be die shaped. Other shapes have risen in value, too, thanks to the idea that each one serves a different purpose. The women come to the market and sweet-talk their fat-walleted merchant and farmer husbands into buying them the stuff. And if you want to talk about miracles, they're even starting to compete among each other, these women, to see who's been given the most pyrite. It's gotten to where the price rises with every word of flattery a woman speaks."

Lawrence had bought wine and trinkets for town girls before; this was difficult for him to hear.

But that difficulty paled in comparison to his regret at having let this opportunity get away.

"It's not a question of what percentage of profit can be made on an investment now. It's a question of how many times, how many *tens* of times you'll *multiply* your money. Your Philip the Third has his eye on your princess, and he's making tremendous amounts of money to get her."

If Amati had come up with this plan as soon as he'd bought Holo her piece of pyrite, he might very well have made a fair amount of money already. It was entirely possible he would have the thousand pieces of silver on the morrow.

"I've just barely gotten my foot in the door, and I've already made three hundred *irehd*. That's how much the price is going up. It's not an opportunity to let go."

"Who else knows?"

"Apparently, it was spreading around the market this morning.

I was actually late to the game. Incidentally, the line in front of the ore merchant's stall was going mad just about the time you were dancing with your princess."

Despite being long-since sober, Lawrence's face was redder than the still-drinking Mark's.

It was not because Mark teased him about Holo, but rather because just when even the dullest of traders would have known to get in on the action, Lawrence had been right next to the marketplace, dancing the night away.

No amount of red-faced frustration could adequately express his feelings.

He was a failure as a merchant.

For the first time since the Ruvinheigen debacle, he wanted to hold his head in his hands and cry.

"If Amati were doing something complicated, there would probably be something we could do to block him. As it is, I don't think we can. I'm sorry, friend, but you're a fish in a barrel here."

Mark was trying to say, *All you can do is wait to be cooked*, but that wasn't what depressed Lawrence. He was simply upset with himself for putting fun with Holo before business.

"Ah, I should mention that the news has already spread through the market, so the number of merchants looking to buy up pyrite to sell has driven the price even higher. What I'm saying is that the wind is just now picking up. If you don't hoist your sail, you'll regret it for the rest of your life."

"True enough. I'll not sit by and watch those ships sail away."

"That's the spirit! And hey, if worst comes to worst, you'll need money to buy a new princess, eh?"

Lawrence smiled wryly at Mark. It would be a good opportunity to make up for his losses in Ruvinheigen at least.

"In that case, I'll just use some of my credit with you from those nails to take that pyrite off your hands," said Lawrence.

Mark immediately scowled as if he suddenly regretted mentioning anything.

Lawrence paid Mark thirty *trenni* for four pieces of pyrite and then made his way back to the inn through the crowds that sang and danced by the light of the bonfires.

The festival seemed to have entered its second stage, and he heard the sound of drums powerfully beaten.

The crowds were dense enough that it was difficult to see, but in contrast to the festivities of the day, the revelry seemed to have become wilder. Straw puppets collided with one another and sword dancers whirled.

It was a surprising development since people had already been dancing and drinking all day long.

But if he wanted to view the festival, it would be easy to do so from the front-row seat that was the inn room.

He hurried through the throng and made for the inn.

Lawrence had some thinking to do.

Amati's chances of actually pulling together a thousand *trenni* had increased, but Lawrence still didn't feel perturbed or worried about losing Holo.

What he worried about was how much he could make with the pyrite he had on hand and how cheaply he could convince Holo to sell him the piece she'd gotten from Amati.

Sometimes worthless items turned into gold.

Festivals were special times indeed.

Along the quieter alleys slightly removed from the clamor and lights of the festival, knights and mercenaries made passes at girls or draped their arms around the already-convinced.

The girls who leaned so easily into the arms of dark-eyed, dangerous, bandit-like knights did not seem to be women of the night, but rather ordinary town girls, who on any other night would only speak to men of more serious disposition and stature.

The strange aphrodisiac that was the passionate festival atmosphere clouded their eyes — and so long as it also did things like drive the price of pyrite upward, Lawrence had no complaints.

As he was mulling this over, Lawrence caught sight of a shop selling sweet melons to soothe throats burning from too much wine and bought two for Holo.

There was no telling how angry she might be should he return empty-handed. The melons were like the eggs of some huge bird; he smiled, resigned, carrying one under his arm and one in his hand.

The inn's first-floor dining hall was just as lively as the streets, but Lawrence only glanced at it as he made his way up to the second story.

Upon reaching the second floor, Lawrence noticed that the noise from below seemed strangely unreal, as though he were watching a fire burn from the opposite shore.

The sound of the chatter brought to mind a babbling brook; he listened to it as he opened the door and entered the room.

For a moment, he wondered why it was so well lit, but then he saw that the window had been left open.

It had probably been too dark to read the letter otherwise.

Suddenly, Lawrence realized something was wrong with that notion.

The letter?

He met Holo's eyes as she stood before the window with the letter in her hand.

Those frightened eyes.

No — not frightened.

The eyes of someone who had just come back to their senses after being utterly stunned.

"You…"

…*can read?* Lawrence was going to ask, but the words stuck in his throat.

Holo's lips quivered, followed shortly by her shoulders. He saw her try to gather strength in her numb, slim fingers, but the letter slipped from them and fluttered to the floor.

Lawrence did not move. He was afraid she would shatter like an ice sculpture if he moved.

It was the letter from Diana that she'd held.

If reading that letter brought Holo to this state, there were not many possibilities Lawrence could imagine.

It had to be about Yoitsu.

"Whatever is the matter?" she asked.

Her voice sounded as it always did. Despite being visibly on the brink of collapse, she managed a thin smile; the contrast was unreal, dreamlike.

"Is there something s-stuck to my face?" Holo tried maintaining her smile, but her lips trembled and it was clearly difficult for her to speak.

Lawrence looked into her eyes, which were unfocused.

"There's nothing on your face. You might be a bit drunk, though."

He couldn't bear standing silently before her like that, so he tried to choose the least offensive words he could.

What to say next? No, he had to figure out first how much she knew. Lawrence had gotten that far when Holo spoke again.

"Y-yes, quite. I-I must be drunk. Drunk i-indeed."

Her teeth chattered as she smiled, and she stiffly walked over to the bed and sat.

Lawrence finally moved away from the door and very slowly, so as not to cause this frightened bird to fly, made his way to the desk.

He set the two melons down on the desk and casually glanced down at the letter Holo had dropped.

Diana's lovely handwriting was clearly illuminated by the moonlight.

> *Regarding the matter we discussed yesterday of the town*
> *of Yoitsu, destroyed long ago...*

Lawrence's eyes flicked over the words. He couldn't help closing his eyes.

Holo had claimed to be unable to read—probably she had planned to surprise or to tease him sometime in the future. No doubt she was surprised that the chance to do so had come so quickly, and she had read the letter immediately.

But it had backfired.

The letter had been about her home of Yoitsu—of course, she would want to read it.

The image of an excited Holo tearing into the envelope suddenly flickered into Lawrence's mind.

And then she saw the words about Yoitsu's destruction. He couldn't even imagine how bad the shock must have been.

Holo sat on the bed, staring at the floor.

While Lawrence struggled to think of the right words, she looked up.

"What—what shall I do?" Her lips curled into a forced smile. "I've...I've nowhere to return to..."

She neither blinked nor cried, but a steady stream of tears rolled down her cheeks.

"What shall I do...," she murmured again, like a child who had broken her favorite toy. Lawrence couldn't bear to see her this way. Everyone was a child when they remembered their homelands.

Holo was a wisewolf of many centuries' experience; she had certainly considered the possibility that Yoitsu had been buried within the flow of time.

But just as logic has no hold over a child, it was of no use in the face of such strong emotions.

"Holo."

Holo flinched momentarily at the sound of her name before regaining some composure.

"It's just an old story, a legend. There are many legends that are mistaken."

Lawrence spoke almost admonishingly, in order to give his words as much weight as he could. As far as possibilities went, the chances of Yoitsu being intact were very low. The towns that survived unharmed for hundreds of years were typically large ones; that everyone knew.

But he could think of nothing else to say.

"Mis...mistaken?"

"That's right. In places where a new king or faction takes over, they'll spread all kinds of tales like this to stake a claim to the new territory."

It wasn't a lie. He had heard many such examples of this.

But Holo shook her head suddenly, her tears streaming left and right across her cheeks.

The stillness in her eyes was the calm before the storm.

"No, if that were true, why — why would you hide it from me?"

"I was looking for the right time to speak. It's a delicate issue. So —"

"Heh," Holo laughed, though it sounded like a cough.

It was as though a demon had possessed her somehow.

"I-It must have been terribly amusing, seeing me be so carefree."

Lawrence's mind went instantly blank. He could never feel anything of the sort. Anger surged up within him, seizing his throat, but he restrained it somehow.

He realized Holo just wanted to hurt something, *anything*.

"Holo, please, calm down."

"I'm qu-quite calm. Am I not the very picture of lucidity? You must have known about Yoitsu all along."

Lawrence was speechless; she had discerned the truth.

He realized that his ultimate mistake lay in hiding it from her.

"You did, did you not? Did you not? You knew as soon as you met me. That explains so much."

Holo's expression was now that of a cornered wolf.

"Hah. Y-you like sad, weak little lambs. So how was I, as I talked of returning to the homeland you knew was destroyed? Was I foolish enough? Charming enough? Was I sad and lovely enough? So much so that you'd forgive my selfishness and take pity on me?"

Lawrence tried to speak, but Holo continued.

"And then you told me to go back to Nyohhira alone because you'd grown tired of me, no?"

Her smile was a despairing one. Even Holo herself should know that what she said was a deliberate, malicious distortion.

He knew that if he was to lose his temper and strike her, she would only wag her tail happily.

"Is that really what you think?"

Lawrence's words struck her; she stared through him with blazing red eyes. "Yes, it is!"

Holo stood up, her fists trembling and white.

Her sharp teeth clattered, and her tail puffed out like a bottle-brush.

Lawrence still did not flinch. He knew that Holo's rage came from a place of deep sadness.

"Yes, I do think that! You are human! The only animal that raises other animals! It must have been so amusing for you as I foolishly took the bait that was Yoitsu and—"

"Holo."

Holo had been gesticulating wildly; Lawrence quickly drew close to her and grabbed her arms with all his might.

She was as angry and frightened as a trapped stray dog, and she could put up no more resistance than that of the young girl she appeared to be.

With Lawrence holding on to her arms, the difference in their strength was clear.

"I-I'm all alone. Wh-what shall I-I do? No one awaits my return. There is no one for me. I'm…I'm alone…"

"You have me, don't you?" he said, completely serious.

They were not words that could be said lightly.

But Holo merely scoffed and shot back, "What are you to me? Nay—what am I to you?"

Lawrence had no quick reply. He had to think.

It was a moment later that he realized he should have answered quickly, even if it had to be a lie.

"No! I do not want to be alone anymore! I can't!" shouted Holo, then froze. "Come now…Would…would you lie with me?"

Lawrence was just about to loosen his grip on her arms.

But then he noticed that her smile was empty. She was mocking her own unhinged state.

"I am all alone, I am. But with a child, that would make two. Look, I have taken human form. It is not impossible that with you, I could…Come, please…"

"Don't talk. I'm begging you."

Lawrence understood the overflowing emotions that boiled up within her, which could only come out as sharp, poisonous words. He understood too well.

But he could not manage the trick of tying those emotions up and setting them aside to cool.

Telling her not to speak was all he could do.

Holo's smile strengthened, and a new wave of tears poured from her eyes.

"Heh. Aha…ha-ha-ha-ha. 'Tis true. You're too softhearted. I

can expect nothing like that from you. But I care not. I've remembered, you see. There's . . . Yes, there's someone who loves me."

She couldn't overcome Lawrence's grip with force, so in order to take advantage of any gap that might appear, Holo relaxed her fists and let the tension drain from her body. Lawrence let go of her wrists, and words now came from her like so many sickly butterflies.

"That is why such talk did not cause you worry, is it not? That if you could receive a thousand silver coins for me, it would not be so regrettable to let me go?"

Lawrence knew that anything he said would be meaningless, so he only listened silently.

The silence continued, as if Holo had burned up the last of her fuel.

At length, just when Lawrence reached out to her again, Holo spoke weakly.

". . . I am sorry," she said.

Lawrence felt he could hear the *slam* that came with those words as Holo closed the door to her heart.

He froze. It was all he could do to back away.

Holo sat down again, staring at the floor, unmoving.

Lawrence retreated, but he found himself unable to stand still, so he picked up the letter from Diana that Holo had dropped, reading it as if to escape.

In it, Diana said that there was a monk who lived in a town on the way to Lenos, specializing in the legends of the northlands, and that Lawrence would do well to visit him. On the back of the letter was written the name of the monk.

Lawrence closed his eyes, anguished.

If only he had looked at the letter first. If only.

He was filled with a sudden urge to tear it into pieces, but he knew such an outburst was pointless.

The letter was still an important clue to finding Yoitsu.

It felt like one of the few thin threads still connecting Holo to him; he folded the letter and slipped it beneath his coat.

He looked back at Holo, who still stared at the floor.

In his mind, he heard again the word she had spoken — "sorry" — when he reached out to her.

All he could do now was silently leave the room.

He took one step back. Two steps.

A loud cheer came through the window. Lawrence took this opportunity and left the room.

For just an instant, he thought that Holo had lifted her face to look at him, but he knew it was just hope's illusion.

He reached behind himself to close the door, averting his eyes as if to make it clear he wished to see nothing.

But that would not undo all of this.

He would have to do something.

He would have to do something — but what and how?

Lawrence left the inn.

The streets were again overflowing with strangers.

CHAPTER FOUR

Lawrence headed out into the town only to find there was no place for him there.

The festival that had started when the sun set was the precise opposite of its daytime counterpart, and it lacked the latter's sense of fun entirely.

Every straw or wooden puppet was now armed with a weapon, to say nothing of every costumed reveler. The larger puppets that had no weapons were themselves used *as* weapons as the fighting spread.

The straw puppets collided amid angry cries, the crowds yelling each time debris went flying. Around them instruments blared their raucous tunes so as not to be drowned out by the clamor of fighting. The black-robed figures sang an ominous war hymn.

Lawrence avoided the crowds and headed north. The awful din churned over and over in his head unbearably.

No matter how long he walked down the long avenue, the festival noise seemed endless. It ate into his nerves like some witch's spell, causing his exchange with Holo to echo through his mind. He could see her before him. He wanted to cry out at his own worthlessness but managed to restrain himself.

If he had enough energy to scream, Lawrence reasoned, he should put that toward improving the situation.

Yet evaluating the situation rationally, he could find no such possibilities.

Given the state Holo was in, Lawrence saw it was entirely possible that she would accept Amati's proposal.

Amati was probably the first merchant to have taken advantage of the pyrite boom, so it was best to assume that he had already made a fair amount of money.

In the worst case, Amati might not even have to wait until sunset to bring the money and declare the contract fulfilled.

Lawrence knew he was not just being pessimistic.

"..."

The anxiety seized his gut, and a whimper escaped his lips.

He looked up into the dark sky and covered his eyes.

If he couldn't stop Amati's profit machine, he could at least go back to the inn and try to make up with Holo.

But Lawrence could see plain as day that reconciling with Holo would be even more difficult than stopping Amati.

What am I to you? Holo's question had thrown him into contemplation.

Even now, having had a bit of time to consider the question, he could not answer it.

He wanted her to keep traveling with him — that much he knew — and he couldn't bear even thinking about her going to be Amati's bride.

Yet after ruminating on the memory of the scene, his face only contorted at the terrible acidity of it.

He knew that Holo was precious to him, but precious in what way? If asked, it was not something he could articulate clearly.

His jaw was clenched, and Lawrence rubbed his face to try and relax it.

How could this have happened?

The fun they'd had at the festival now seemed like a fleeting dream. Even an omniscient god could never have anticipated that in a few short hours, things would turn out this way.

Ahead of him, Lawrence saw a procession of sword dancers moving down the street. The savage, sinister atmosphere was completely changed from the daytime revels. It echoed the shift in Lawrence's relationship with Holo, and he quickened his step, averting his eyes.

He regretted leaving the letter on the desk. It felt to him like none of this would have happened if he had only taken it with him. If he had only found the right time to talk to her, surely the clever Holo would not have become distraught.

Beyond that, Holo's words had laid bare his own selfishness and lack of resolve. He couldn't imagine being able to speak to her properly now.

Eventually Lawrence realized he'd made it all the way to Kumersun's lonely northern district without having come up with any good ideas.

He'd been walking slowly, and it had taken some time, but he hadn't even noticed.

Despite the sense that the town was crowded everywhere one might go, here in the northern section there were few pedestrians. The festivities did not extend this far.

There in the silence, he was finally able to calm down and take some deep breaths.

He turned on his heel and began to walk back, rethinking the situation.

First —

Sincerity alone would not be enough to convince Holo to hear him out. He didn't even have enough confidence to look her in the eye anyway.

So setting aside whether or not he would be able to salvage his relationship with her, he could at least avoid giving her a good reason to leave him and be with Amati.

As long as Amati was unable to raise a thousand silver pieces, Holo's debt to Lawrence would still stand. There was no telling if that would be enough to get her to stay with him, but he could at least try to make that assertion.

So the problem lay in preventing Amati from fulfilling the contract.

It was due to the strange mood of the festival that the price of pyrite had risen so high, and to hear Mark tell it, the price was going to rise still higher. Lawrence did not know how much pyrite Amati had on hand or how much profit he had turned. Since the pyrite was selling for many times — even many *tens* of times — its cost price, depending on how much money Amati had been able to invest, he might already have raised the thousand silver.

However, there was a factor that worked in Lawrence's favor — pyrite did tend to exist in large quantities.

Even if it could be sold for ten times the purchase price, one had to have the pyrite in quantity before making truly large amounts of money.

Of course, Amati wasn't necessarily relying solely on pyrite to raise the money, but the thought that he might have trouble obtaining sufficient quantity to do so was some consolation to Lawrence.

Lawrence had to prevent Amati from making this kind of deal. More accurately, he had to force him to take a loss, because if Amati was pressed and didn't care about the future of his business, he might liquidate all of his assets just to raise the money.

But if Lawrence found it difficult to stop him from turning a huge profit, forcing him to suffer a loss was nearly impossible.

A frontal assault was out of the question. The rising demand for

pyrite meant there was no need to push any deals through by force; the profit would naturally come.

If there was no urgency, there was no way to swindle.

So what to do...?

He turned the problem over and over in his mind, always running into the same walls. Eventually without thinking, Lawrence said, "Say, Ho —"

He managed not to say "lo," but a passing craftsman did look at him strangely.

Again, he realized how largely Holo's small figure and invincible smile loomed in his mind.

It seemed impossible that he'd gotten along on his own for so long before her.

Holo would certainly be able to come up with some good ideas or at least set him on the right path.

Somewhere along the line, Lawrence realized, he'd become quite dependent on her.

What am I to you?

He simply could not answer the question with any kind of confidence.

"If I were Holo, what would I do?"

Lawrence didn't imagine that he could imitate the endlessly mysterious Holo's thought process perfectly.

But he was a merchant.

When a merchant came upon a new idea, it was his job to make that idea his own and get ahead of his competitors.

Holo always considered every facet of a situation.

Given the situation before him, Lawrence knew she would look at the whole problem from every possible angle.

It seemed easy but wasn't. Sometimes the most brilliant idea would seem obvious in retrospect.

Amati was making a profit on the rising demand for pyrite. Lawrence needed to make him suffer a loss.

What was the simplest, most obvious way for that to happen? Lawrence mused.

Unconstrained by the bonds of common sense, he thought.

One answer occurred to him.

"The demand for pyrite needs to fall."

Lawrence said it out loud, then laughed foolishly.

So this is what happened when he tried to imitate Holo?

If the value of pyrite was to drop, that truly would be cause for celebration.

But demand was climbing and showed no signs of stopping. The price was already past increases of tenfold, twentyfold. It would climb and then —

"…And then?"

Lawrence stopped dead in his tracks as the realization hit him.

"Ten times? Twenty times? And then what…thirty? And after that?"

He felt as if he could see Holo snickering at him.

The price would not rise forever. The craze would end as it always did.

Lawrence almost felt like he might sob again. He clamped his hand over his mouth to stifle it.

There were two questions he had to answer:

The first was when the crash would come, and the second was would it be possible to make Amati fall with it?

Lawrence started walking again, his hand still over his mouth.

Even if the price of pyrite were to crash, would Amati really be pulled down with it? Lawrence doubted it. It would be underestimating the boy to assume so.

So the problem would be contriving to make that situation

happen. If he could articulate the problem concretely, Lawrence didn't think his mind was so very far behind Holo's.

The ideal situation appeared in his mind, settling heavy and cold into his stomach. He'd experienced this sensation before. It wasn't logic, but the intuition that an important contest was upon him.

He took a deep breath and thought about a critical point: When would the crash occur?

It was obvious that the price could not continue to rise forever, but when would it crash — and more to the point, would it crash sometime before the end of the next day, when the contract between Lawrence and Amati was up?

Even a fortune-teller would find it impossible to predict such a thing, as would anyone short of the gods themselves.

Lawrence pictured in his mind the farmers in a wheat-producing region, using their own ingenuity to carry out the harvests that had once been the sole purview of the gods.

Rather than waiting terrified for the gods to make the price drop, why not become those gods?

A moment after the outrageous arrogance of the idea occurred to him, a great cry arose, and he turned to look.

Lawrence realized that he'd walked all the way back into town and arrived again at the center of the great intersection.

The straw puppets still collided with one another amid angry shouts, each collision bringing a shower of twigs and cries. It was like an actual war.

Lawrence set aside his scheming for a moment to appreciate the intensity of the scene, and he saw something that immediately brought him back to his senses.

He felt the hairs on the back of his neck stand up.

Amati.

Amati was right there.

At first he thought it was some cruel joke of the gods, but

then he wondered — even this coincidence might be somehow significant.

Lawrence stood in the heart of Kumersun at the intersection of the main streets running north to south and east to west.

Amati's back was toward the inn where Holo presumably still was.

Amati stopped and slowly looked behind him.

For a moment, Lawrence was afraid that Amati saw him, but no, Amati didn't notice him at all.

Lawrence followed the boy's gaze.

Its direction was obvious.

But what was there? Lawrence had to know.

And there, at a window on the second floor of the inn, facing the broad avenue, fox skin muffler wrapped about her neck, was Holo.

A terrible anxiety roiled in Lawrence's stomach that was bitter with anger and a kind of impatience.

Holo nuzzled the muffler and then nodded.

Lawrence saw Amati put his hand over his chest in response, as though swearing an oath before God.

Whether Holo had invited him in or Amati had forced his way in, Lawrence did not know.

However, based on what he was seeing, Lawrence thought there was little reason to be optimistic.

Amati turned his back on the inn and walked away. He leaned forward and seemed hurried, as though he was escaping, which only exacerbated Lawrence's suspicions.

In a moment, Amati had disappeared into the crowd, and Lawrence looked back to the inn window.

He held his breath.

Holo was clearly looking directly at him.

If Lawrence was able to spot Amati in the crowd, there was no reason the sharp-eyed Holo would have difficulty spotting Lawrence.

Although Holo did not look away immediately, neither did she smile. She simply looked at him steadily.

They stayed that way for some time. Lawrence was about to finally exhale when Holo suddenly withdrew from the windowsill.

If she had closed the window, he might have stayed frozen there. But she didn't. The window was left open.

It seemed to exert a pull on him, drawing him toward the inn.

Lawrence was of course not so naive as to think that Holo and Amati had simply spoken through the window.

Holo was no simple town girl, and Amati's feelings for her were far from coolheaded. There was no reason to think that they hadn't had a conversation in the room.

Holo had looked quietly unflustered and unconcerned, probably because she hadn't been seen doing anything she would need to be concerned about.

Which meant she was provoking him.

Lawrence thought back to the conversation they had once had in Ruvinheigen. He believed that if he spoke to her honestly, she would understand.

He steeled himself and then headed for the inn.

Immediately upon entering the inn, Lawrence was greeted by a lively feast.

The tables were piled with all manner of food, and the guests were drinking, talking, and even singing.

It occurred to Lawrence that he and Holo should have been at one of those tables enjoying themselves, and despite his merchant's aversion to regret, he felt a pang nonetheless.

But there was still a chance. If Holo had wanted to utterly reject him, she would've closed the window.

Lawrence held onto that tenuous idea, which gave him confidence, and ascended the stairs next to the counter, leading to the second floor.

Immediately, someone called out to him.

"Mr. Lawrence—"

Not particularly serene to begin with, Lawrence started and turned around; the innkeeper was also surprised, blinking as he looked at Lawrence while leaning over the counter.

"...I'm sorry, is there something...?"

"Ah, yes, I was told to give you a letter."

The mention of a letter sent a surge of uneasiness through Lawrence's chest. He stifled it with a cough.

Descending the stairs, he walked over to the counter and took the proffered letter.

"Who is this from?"

"Your companion left it just a moment ago."

Impressively, Lawrence managed to hide his surprise.

It went without saying that the innkeeper had knowledge of all the comings and goings of his inn's residents.

Lawrence had left the inn, and Holo had remained. While Lawrence was out, Amati paid Holo a visit, and Holo now chose to communicate with Lawrence not directly but via letter.

No innkeeper could observe these events and not suppose something was afoot.

Yet the innkeeper betrayed no such suspicions as he looked at Lawrence.

Connections between merchants in a town like this ran deeply.

If Lawrence was to behave in an unseemly fashion here, the rumors would be all over town almost instantly.

"Might I borrow a light?" Lawrence said with careful control. The innkeeper nodded and brought out a silver candlestick from the back.

The bright candle was not tallow, and Lawrence felt that his inner turmoil might be laid bare underneath its strong light.

In his mind, he smiled derisively at himself for entertaining such thoughts, and then he cut open the envelope with the dagger at his waist.

The innkeeper moved away, as if realizing it would be rude of him to read the contents of the letter, but Lawrence could tell the man still glanced at him from time to time.

He coughed lightly and removed the letter from its envelope.

One sheet was parchment; the other was normal paper.

His heart pounded. Hesitating here meant that he did not completely trust Holo.

It was well within the realm of possibility that within the letter, Holo would attempt reconciliation.

He opened the letter — which was folded in half — slowly, and a bit of sand fell from the surface of the paper.

It had probably been used in order to persuade the ink to dry more quickly, which meant the letter had only just been written.

Would it be a letter that repaired their relationship or destroyed it?

The words on the paper leapt out at Lawrence's eyes.

Cash on hand, two hundred silver pieces. Pyrite on hand, three hundred silver pieces' worth. Salable assets —

He looked up, taken aback at the list of assets that began without so much as a preamble.

Cash? Pyrite?

He had expected a letter that would echo in his mind with her voice, but what he held here was a sheet of paper with a list of figures and nothing more.

Lawrence looked back to the paper and, gritting his teeth, continued reading.

*...on hand, three hundred silver pieces' worth. Salable
assets roughly two hundred silver pieces' worth.*

This was obviously a list of Amati's assets.

Lawrence felt his shoulders slacken, as if they were stale bread
loaves sprinkled with water.

Holo had allowed Amati into the room so she could get this
information from him.

She had to have done so for Lawrence.

It was her roundabout way of reconciling.

Lawrence smiled widely. He didn't even bother trying to hide it.

At the end of the note was written "*These contents transcribed
by another.*"

There were many people who could read but not write. Holo
had gotten this information, slipped from the room under the
pretense of visiting the restroom perhaps, and gotten a merchant
or someone to write out the list for her. Lawrence remembered
Amati's handwriting from the contract. This was not his writing.

Lawrence carefully folded up the note, which was now suddenly
beyond value to him, and tucked it near his breast, and then he
pulled the parchment free.

Perhaps she'd used her wiles to fool Amati into signing some
sort of ridiculous contract.

Lawrence flashed to the memory of Amati's self-satisfied face
after his meeting with Holo.

Holo still wants to travel with me, Lawrence thought to himself.

Flooded with a sense of incredible relief, he unfolded the parchment without hesitation.

In the name of God...

It was unmistakably Amati's bold, gallant handwriting.

Lawrence quashed the rush of emotion that came and kept reading.

He read the first line, the second line, the third line —

And then —

By these terms shall the two be bound in marriage.

As he got to the end of the document, it felt like the world was spinning around him.

"...Wha...?"

He heard himself murmur in a voice that sounded very faraway indeed.

He closed his eyes, but the contents of the parchment, the words that he'd just read, remained there in his vision.

It was a marriage certificate.

There on the parchment, sworn in the name of God, were written the names of a young fishmonger named Fermi Amati and Holo.

The line for the signature of Holo's guardian was blank.

But once it had been signed and sealed by her guardian and delivered to a church, Amati and Holo would be husband and wife.

Holo's name had been written in an uncertain hand.

Hers were the letters of someone who could read but who could only write by imitation.

An image flashed through Lawrence's mind — Holo watching Amati write the contract and then clumsily signing her own name.

Lawrence pulled the first sheet of paper out of his breast pocket — that desperately valuable paper — and reread it.

It had to be a list of Amati's property. The amounts were entirely plausible.

She must have composed the list not to help Lawrence, but rather to show him just how dire the situation was.

Why would she do that? It was silly even to ask.

Taken along with the marriage certificate, Lawrence thought the answer was obvious.

Amati was on the verge of fulfilling his contract with Lawrence, whom Holo was planning to leave.

Their meeting, Holo's and Lawrence's, had been pure chance.

Despite Amati being young, rash, and honest to a fault, Holo had perhaps found the overachieving, self-important boy to be a more suitable partner.

There was no reason not to think so.

Even if Lawrence was to dash up the stairs and beg her not to marry, clutching the marriage certificate in his hand, Holo would simply turn him out. She excelled at that.

He had no choice but to steel himself.

Holo had revealed Amati's assets to Lawrence; she had to be telling him that if he could successfully defeat the young fishmonger, she would hear him out. On the other hand, if Lawrence failed — that would be the end of it.

There was a way to defeat Amati. There was hope.

Lawrence quickly put the note and contract away, and then he turned to the innkeeper.

"Fetch me all the coin I've left with you, if you please."

Traveling with Holo was worth all the gold he'd ever have.

Lawrence knew it was possible to legally bankrupt Amati.

The problem lay in getting Amati to accept a deal that held such a possibility.

Lawrence suspected Amati was unfamiliar with the sort of deal he would propose. This wasn't because he looked down on the boy; it was simply because Amati's business did not involve transactions like the one that Lawrence had in mind.

Nobody wants to get involved in deals they don't fully understand, after all.

Lawrence had the additional disadvantage of being Amati's enemy.

Given all that, he expected the odds of Amati accepting his deal at one in nine on the outside. Lawrence didn't care if he had to provoke the boy — he had to get Amati to take the bait.

Unfortunately, no matter how normal the deal appeared on the surface, Amati was bound to notice how antagonistic it really was.

The provocation Lawrence considered was thus entirely justified.

This was not business because Lawrence had no intention of turning a profit.

Any time a merchant's thoughts strayed from gains and losses, losses were inevitable. But Lawrence had long since abandoned his merchant's common sense.

He asked the innkeeper which taverns Amati frequented and began searching them one by one. Despite the festivities that continued in the streets, he found Amati quietly drinking alone.

The boy appeared fatigued; perhaps it was the aftermath from the tension of negotiating his hoped-for marriage with Holo, or perhaps he had not yet raised the thousand silver pieces.

In any case, Amati's emotional state was completely irrelevant.

Lawrence knew he couldn't always count on completely favorable negotiation conditions. When it came to that, a merchant had only his own abilities to fall back on.

If he waited until tomorrow, the negotiations could become even more difficult.

The deal he was going to propose to Amati could not wait.

He took a deep breath and moved into Amati's field of vision before the latter noticed him.

"Ah —"

"Good evening."

Amati was apparently not so naive as to betray his irritation at Lawrence's arrival.

He was surprised enough to be speechless for a moment, but the young fishmonger soon recovered his professional demeanor.

"No need for suspicion. I'm here for business." Lawrence surprised himself by managing an easy smile.

"If you're here on business, it's all the more reason not to let down my guard," said Amati, unamused.

"Ha-ha, fair enough. Can you spare a moment?"

Amati nodded, and Lawrence sat down at the table with him. "Wine," Lawrence simply said to the annoyed-looking tavern keeper.

Lawrence reminded himself not to underestimate the slender, effeminate boy who sat across the table from him. Amati had left his home and and was on his way to success with his fish-selling business.

At the same time, he could not let Amati keep his own guard up.

Lawrence cleared his throat casually, glancing around before speaking. "This is a nice, quiet place."

"You can't drink peacefully at most taverns. This place is special."

Lawrence wondered if Amati was implying that his peace had been disturbed by a certain unpleasant character, that is, himself, but decided that was overthinking.

He was of one mind with Amati in that he wanted to finish the conversation as quickly as possible.

"So I know you must be surprised to see me but no more surprised than I was earlier today, so I think I can beg your indulgence."

Lawrence didn't know what Amati had said to get Holo to sign the contract. No matter how clever and impulsive she was, he could not imagine what would make her actually sign.

Which meant that Amati had somehow persuaded her, and she had agreed.

However, Lawrence knew he had no right to blame her.

The one who had let Amati into the room was Holo, but the one who had caused the situation in the first place was Lawrence.

He did not know then what Holo had heard from Amati. Amati opened his mouth to explain just that presumably, but Lawrence raised his hand and cut the boy off.

"No, that is not the matter I am here to discuss. It does however inform my decision to come and talk business with you certainly, but that is all. Holo is entirely free to act as she will."

Amati looked at Lawrence angrily for a moment and then nodded.

He was clearly still suspicious of Lawrence, but for his part, Lawrence would expend no more effort to allay those suspicions.

After all, what he was going to say next would only heighten them.

"However, given the reason for my proposing this deal to you, I can't very well call it normal."

"Just what is it you're scheming?" Amati asked.

Unfazed, Lawrence continued, "I'll get right to the point, then. It is my wish to sell you pyrite."

Amati's blue eyes seemed to look through Lawrence into some far-off place for a moment. "What?"

"I wish to sell you pyrite. By current market value, it is roughly five hundred silver pieces' worth."

Amati, mouth half-open and eyes unfocused, regained his composure. He laughed and then sighed. "Surely you jest."

"I am quite serious."

Amati's smile disappeared, his keen eyes now almost angry. "You must be aware that I have done quite well reselling pyrite. What are you playing at, trying to sell it then to *me*? The more I have, the more money I can make. I cannot believe you would help me in this. Unless" — Amati paused, his gaze now definitely angry — "it's true that as long as you collect the debt, you care not what becomes of Miss Holo."

"Far from it. Holo is very important to me."

"In that case, why —"

"Of course, I do not mean to simply sell it to you outright."

Amati might have been the better man when it came to the frenetic business of auctions, but when negotiating one-on-one, Lawrence had confidence in his own abilities.

Keeping his tone even, he continued on with his proposal.

"I wish to sell it to you on margin."

"On...margin?" Amati repeated the unfamiliar phrase.

"Quite."

"And what does that —"

"It means I will sell you five hundred *trenni* of pyrite tomorrow evening at its current market value."

Holo sometimes bragged of being able to hear the sound of someone frowning in consternation — Lawrence now felt he heard that very sound, so complete was Amati's look of non-comprehension.

"In that case, simply come to me tomorrow evening —"

"No, I'd like to receive the payment now."

Amati's dubious expression grew still more dubious.

Unless he was as good at acting as Holo, Amati obviously knew nothing of margin selling.

A merchant that lacked knowledge might as well be entering a battlefield while blindfolded.

Lawrence pulled his bowstring tight, preparing to fire his arrow.

"In other words, I'll accept five hundred silver pieces from you now, and tomorrow I'll give you five hundred silver pieces' worth of pyrite at today's market value."

Amati thought hard. On the surface, it was not a difficult arrangement to understand.

After a time, he seemed to work out the implications.

"So what this means is that come tomorrow evening, even if the market value of pyrite has risen, I'll still receive what I would have gotten at today's price."

"Correct. For example, if I sold you a single piece of pyrite worth twelve hundred *irehd* on margin tonight, even if tomorrow's price is two thousand *irehd*, I still have to give you the pyrite."

"…Contrariwise, if the value has dropped to two hundred *irehd* by tomorrow, I still receive only the one piece, despite having paid twelve hundred the night before."

"Also correct."

The boy was clever.

However, Lawrence still worried whether Amati would understand the true meaning of margin transactions.

In a sense, they were no different from when a merchant sold a commodity on the spot.

If the price of a good was to rise after it had been sold, a merchant would regret not waiting to sell it. Likewise, if it fell, he would be relieved at having gotten a better deal.

But the time interval between the cash transaction and the commodity transaction was an important one.

Lawrence wanted Amati to understand this.

If Amati failed to see the significance of it, he would in all likelihood turn down the proposal.

Amati spoke.

"How is this different from an ordinary transaction?"

He did not understand.

Lawrence stifled the urge to click his tongue in irritation and prepared to deliver a lecture on margin purchasing.

Just then, Amati cut him off before he could begin.

"No, wait. It *is* different." Amati smiled in understanding, his boyish face now every inch a merchant's, calculating gain and loss. "You, Mr. Lawrence, are trying to salvage some profit despite having arrived late to the game. Am I right?"

It seemed a lecture would be unnecessary.

A merchant would not propose a meaningless deal. It only appeared meaningless when viewed in ignorance.

Amati continued, "If buying on margin allows you to gain a commodity without having the cash on hand, then selling on margin allows you to gain cash without having the commodity on hand. Buying on margin yields profit when the good rises in price, but selling on margin allows you to profit when the good's market value *drops*."

When selling on margin, one did not even need to have the goods on hand until they were due to be delivered, since the deal was made by promising to deliver goods at a later point in time.

"This is quite a business, indeed. It seems my focus on fish has left me ignorant of much of the world. You chose me for this deal because... No, it goes without saying. If I buy five hundred silver pieces' worth of pyrite from you, I stand to gain if the market value of pyrite rises, but if it falls, my losses increase. When you profit — that is when I lose."

Amati thrust out his chest, his face fairly brimming with confidence.

Lawrence was acutely aware of his own even expression.

His hand trembled upon the bowstring.

Amati continued, "So in other words, this is —"

Lawrence cut him off and let fly the arrow.

"Mr. Amati, I am challenging you to a battle."

The fishmonger's lips curled into a smile.

It was every bit a merchant's smile.

"Surely this cannot be called a 'battle.' A battle presupposes that both sides are equal, and this is not equal at all. I'm sure that you're not suggesting that this transaction would be meaningful only between you and me?"

"By which you mean...?"

"Surely you don't plan to conduct the deal without a certificate, and I assume this certificate could be sold to someone else, correct?"

Outside of remote areas, it was quite common for debt obligations to be bought and sold.

Certificates for margin selling were no exception.

"I would hardly expect you to accept my proposal otherwise," replied Lawrence. "It would be far too much risk; you would never accept it."

"Quite so. Even supposing the value of pyrite drops by tomorrow evening as you're predicting it will, as long as it reaches the value I need sometime during the day, I'll want to sell the certificate. If I weren't allowed to do that, I doubt I would accept the deal. But if I keep that ability, the deal remains unfair."

Lawrence listened silently as Amati continued.

"It's unfair to you, Mr. Lawrence, since all I need is a slight increase in the price of pyrite to reach my goal. And yet I cannot accept a deal that leans in your favor."

So either way, Amati was unwilling.

But no merchant worth his salt would give up after a single refusal.

Lawrence calmed himself and replied.

"That may be true if you look at this transaction by itself, but if you'll look at the bigger picture, you'll see this amount of unfairness is actually quite fair."

"...By which you mean...?"

"By which I mean it is quite possible that Holo will simply tear up that marriage certificate. I assume you have a copy as well?"

Amati paled.

"Even if you pay me the thousand silver to lift Holo's debt, there's no way for you to avoid the risk of her simply shaking her head no. Compared to that risk, the marginal unfairness I face is nothing."

"Hah. Don't you think that worry is unfounded? I understand you had quite a row with her," Amati shot back with a snort and a chuckle.

Lawrence felt his body grow hot as though he was empaled from behind on a red-hot iron bar, but he summoned every ounce of his merchant's self-control and revealed nothing. "In our travels together, Holo has cried in my arms three times."

It was now Amati whose face betrayed his emotion.

He'd had a smirk, but his face now froze, and he took a long, slow breath.

"She was quite charming all three times, Holo was," continued Lawrence. "So it's a shame she's usually so stubborn. She often says and does things that are contrary to her true feelings. In other words —"

Amati cut Lawrence off forcefully, like a knight challenged to a duel. "I accept! I accept your proposal, Mr. Lawrence."

"Are you quite sure?"

"I say again: I accept. I was ... if you'll pardon me, I was worried that it would be too cruel to take absolutely everything from you, Mr. Lawrence. But if this is the way you want it, I accept. I will take from you your fortune and everything you have!"

Amati's face was red with anger.

Lawrence had to smile.

As he extended his right hand to Amati, his was the smile of the hunter that reaches into a trap to retrieve his prey. "So you'll accept these terms?"

"I shall!"

The two hands that then clasped tightly together each planned to take everything from the other.

"In that case, let us sign the contract and be done with it."

Lawrence remained coolheaded and came to a conclusion.

The two of them, Lawrence and Amati, were on equal footing when it came to the deal at this time. Amati might even be shouldering a slightly greater risk.

But it was far from clear whether Amati realized this. No, it was precisely because he had *not* realized it that he was willing to agree.

But even if he were to realize now, it would be too late.

They borrowed pen and paper from the tavern keeper and signed the contract on the spot.

Amati couldn't produce five hundred pieces of silver right there, so Lawrence let him substitute his three horses for the remaining two hundred. The coin would be handed over in the morning at the toll of the market bell. The horses would follow in the evening.

If Holo was to be believed, Amati had two hundred silver coins, pyrite worth three hundred pieces of silver, and another two hundred pieces of silver of salable assets.

Evidently, though, he had a hundred more silver pieces than that, and the two hundred silver pieces of salable assets were clearly the three horses.

All this meant that Amati had the equivalent of eight hundred silver pieces' worth of pyrite. If the value of pyrite was to rise by even 25 percent, he'd have more than the thousand silver he needed. If Amati had more assets than what Holo reported, the price wouldn't even need to go up that much.

"We'll settle this tomorrow evening, then," said Amati, visibly excited as the final seal was stamped on the paper. Lawrence nodded calmly.

All he'd had to do was mention Holo crying in his arms.

Merchants truly were useless once matters strayed from business.

"I'll take my leave, then. Enjoy your wine," said Lawrence once the contract was signed and complete.

The arrow was well and truly buried in Amati's chest. Amati himself must have felt it, but there was something Lawrence had failed to mention.

The arrow had been tipped with a slow-acting poison known only to those familiar with margin selling.

The merchant's hunt lay between truth and deception.

There was no obligation to tell the whole truth.

Merchants were all of them treacherous.

As soon as he completed the margin-selling contract with Amati, Lawrence headed straight to the marketplace.

Though business hours were long since over, the marketplace was as lively as it had been during the day. The merchants drank wine and made merry by the light of the moon, and the festivities soon spread to include the night watchmen.

So it was that Mark was still at his stall and not at home as he might have been at such a late hour.

That he was drinking alone, with only the noise of the festivities to accompany the wine, proved he had once been a traveling merchant himself.

"What's this? Does the princess not require an escort?" were the first words from Mark's mouth.

Lawrence shrugged, smiling unhappily.

Mark laughed. "Well, no matter — have a drink," he said, pouring ale from an earthen bottle into an empty cup.

"I'm not disturbing you?"

"You will be if you stay sober!"

Lawrence sat in the sawed-log chair and set down the sack containing the gold and silver coins. He put the proffered ale to his lips. Its foamy fragrance filled his head as the bitter stuff washed down his throat.

The hops had been good in this batch.

Lawrence supposed it was unsurprising that a wheat merchant would know good ale.

"It's fine ale."

"It's been a good harvest this year for all wheat. When there's a bad harvest, the barley that normally goes to ale is put toward bread instead. I'll have to thank the god of the harvest."

"Hah, quite so," said Lawrence, setting the ale cup down on the tabletop. "Listen, this may not be the best discussion to match good ale, but…"

Mark gulped and burped. "Is there profit in it?"

"That's hard to say. There might be gain in it, though that's not my aim."

Mark popped a piece of salted fish into his mouth, speaking as he crunched away on it. "You're too honest, friend. You should've said there's money in it. I'd have gladly helped you."

"I'll pay you for your trouble, and there may yet be profit in it."

"Do tell."

Lawrence wiped a bit of ale foam from the corner of his mouth. "After the festival ends is when the wheat buying begins in earnest, yes?"

"Oh, aye."

"I'd like you to spread a rumor for me."

Mark's expression turned shrewd, as though he was appraising wheat. "I won't do anything risky."

"It might be risky for you to spread it, but your apprentice can do so with no trouble at all."

It was a trifling rumor.

But rumors can wield a terrible power.

There was a tale of a kingdom long ago that met its destruction because of a simple rumor that the king was ill, which was started by a young town boy. The rumor eventually circulated beyond the kingdom's borders, leading to the dissolution of alliances and finally invasion.

It turns out that people do not have that much to talk about in their daily lives.

It seemed that their ears existed only to pick up on small rumors, so they could then shout them to the world.

Mark gestured with his chin, as if to say, "Go on."

"At my signal, I want someone to begin saying that it seems about time for the price of wheat to rise."

Mark froze, his eyes staring through Lawrence and off into the distance. He was considering the implications of what Lawrence had said.

"You're trying to lower the price of that mineral."

"Exactly so."

Lawrence imagined that most of the people who were trying their hand at the pyrite business had come to town to sell something, and they would be buying something before they left.

And as they left, the product they would buy the most of was undoubtedly wheat.

If people heard that wheat was going to rise in price, they would surely sell off their pyrite in order to buy whatever it was they had originally come to town to buy.

And as a result, demand for pyrite would fall off.

As the price fell with less demand, it would reach a certain point and then plunge uncontrollably downward.

The wheat merchant drank deeply from his ale cup before speaking. "I wouldn't have figured you to come up with such a simpleminded idea."

"What if I told you that I was planning to sell off a considerable amount of pyrite at the same time?"

Mark blinked, and after a moment of thought, he asked, "How much?"

"One thousand *trenni* worth."

"Wha —! One thousand? Are you insane? Do you have any idea how much you might lose in the process?"

Mark scowled and scratched his beard, muttering as he looked about. Judging by his reaction, he had no idea what Lawrence was thinking.

"So long as I've five hundred silver pieces' worth of pyrite when this is all over, it matters nothing to me whether the price rises or falls."

It was Amati who had greater risk in the deal Lawrence had brought to him.

And this was the reason.

"Damn. Selling on margin, are you?"

Obviously no one complained when a commodity they had on hand went up in price, but there weren't many situations where someone didn't mind if their goods *dropped* in value.

If the goods sold on margin depreciated, all one had to do was repurchase the product at the new lower price to ensure a profit. If the product rose in value, as long as it were paired up with a conventional transaction, Lawrence could create a situation where he would come out the same whether or not the price rose or fell.

His most decisive advantage was that the price of pyrite would definitely fall once it was sold in large quantities, but Amati absolutely needed the price to rise in order to turn a profit.

Lawrence's plan was, in essence, to use the five hundred silver pieces he'd received from Amati plus his own assets to buy up as much pyrite as possible; then he would sell it off all at once in order to drive the price sharply down.

It was only possible to do this upon abandoning any notion of profit.

Mark, once a traveling merchant himself, soon worked all this out — including who the victim was.

"I must say I feel bad for that poor, ignorant fishmonger."

Lawrence shrugged in reply.

Although the plan looked flawless, there was a reason why Lawrence was not completely comfortable with it.

There was no such thing as a perfect plan.

"You'd think he would understand how dangerous it is to take part in a deal he's not used to," said Mark.

"No — he knows the risks, and he accepted. I explained that much."

Mark gave a throaty chuckle and polished off his beer. "So, was that all you needed?"

"No, there's one more thing."

"I'm all ears."

"I want you to help me buy up pyrite."

Mark stared blankly at Lawrence. "You didn't secure a source before making the margin contract?"

"There wasn't time. Will you help me?"

This was the flaw in his plan.

No matter how ideal the plan, without all the components in place it would come to nothing.

And what Lawrence needed to do was far from easy.

He could wait until dawn to purchase pyrite in the marketplace like any other merchant. But if he bought several hundred *trenni* worth of pyrite all at once, a sudden spike in price was inevitable.

He had to work behind the scenes and buy up pyrite in such a way that his purchasing would not disturb the market value.

To do this, the best way would be to make many small purchases via various town merchants.

"Payments will be in cash. I'll even pay over market value. If the quantity is enough, I can even pay in *lumione*."

If *trenni* silver was a sword, then *lumione* gold was a phalanx of spears. When buying high-value commodities, a more powerful weapon did not exist.

Lawrence had coin but lacked connections, and outside of Mark, he had no one he could turn to for aid.

If Mark refused, Lawrence would have no choice but to gather pyrite on his own.

He couldn't even consider how difficult it would be to buy up the mineral in an aboveboard fashion in this town, where he only did business a few days of the year.

Mark was unmoving, staring off in some unclear direction.

"I'll make it worth your trouble," Lawrence added. It was clear he was offering more than a simple service fee.

Mark glanced over upon hearing those words.

He was, after all, a merchant. He wouldn't work for free.

Mark's answer was short. "I can't."

"I see, so . . . Wait, what?"

"I can't," he said again, looking Lawrence in the eye.

"Wha —"

"I cannot help you with this," he said flatly.

Lawrence leaned forward. "I'll pay you a consideration and not a paltry service fee, either. You've nothing to lose. It's a good trade, is it not?"

"I've nothing to lose?" He frowned, his square-cut beard making his face look even stonier.

"But you don't, do you? I'm asking you to help me find and purchase pyrite, not shoulder a risky investment. What have you to lose?"

"Lawrence." The sound of his name cut Lawrence off.

Yet Lawrence did not understand what Mark was thinking. It made no sense for a merchant to refuse a deal that promised a sizable reward with no risk.

Why then the refusal?

He wondered if Mark was trying to take advantage of him, and something like anger roiled in his gut.

Mark continued, "You'd be able to pay me, say, ten *lumione* at the outside, am I right?"

"Well, given that you're simply making some purchases for me, that's more than generous, I should think. It is not as though I'm asking you to cross a mountain range alone and bring back an entire caravan's worth of ore."

"But you *are* asking me to go about the marketplace and buy up pyrite, are you not? It amounts to the same thing."

"How is that —?" Lawrence stood suddenly, knocking back the log chair with a clatter. He was a moment from bodily grabbing the wheat merchant when he regained his composure.

Mark was unmoved.

His even, businesslike expression did not change.

"Er — I mean, how is that the same thing? I'm hardly asking you to run around all night or to traverse some treacherous mountain pass. I'm simply asking you to help me buy pyrite with your connections."

"It's the same thing, Lawrence," said Mark almost patiently. "You're a traveling merchant who crosses the plains; I do battle in the marketplace. The dangers you see, they're the dangers of the traveling merchant."

"So…" Lawrence swallowed his protest. Mark's face was also strained, as if he'd swallowed something bitter.

Mark continued, "To a town merchant, leaping at every chance to make a quick profit is no virtue. It's making a steady living through an honest, reliable business that makes my reputation, not making big profits on fleeting side jobs. I may be the owner of this stall, but its reputation is not just mine. It extends to my wife, my relatives, and anyone connected with it. If it's making a bit of coin on the side, that's surely not a bad thing…"

Mark paused here, taking another quaff of ale. His knit brow was surely not owing to the ale's bitter taste. "...But helping you find and buy five hundred *trenni* of pyrite is quite another matter. How do you think the townspeople would view me and mine? Would they not think of me as a villain, who cares nothing for his real business and has eyes only on easy riches? Can you pay me enough to take that risk? I was once a traveling merchant myself, and I'd venture to say the trifling sums a traveling merchant handles cannot compare to the amounts town merchants deal with."

Lawrence could say nothing.

Mark made his final statement. "This shop may seem small, but the value of its name is surprisingly high. If the name were to be tarnished, ten or twenty gold pieces would be far from enough to cover it."

It was a compelling statement.

Lawrence had nothing to say in return and stared at the table.

"That's how it is."

Mark was neither taking advantage of Lawrence nor mocking him.

It was simply the truth.

Lawrence saw that though both he and Mark were merchants, they lived in different worlds.

"I am sorry," said Mark.

Lawrence still had no good reply.

It was hardly worth counting the number of allies that remained to him.

"N-no, I should apologize for asking the impossible."

Lawrence tried to think of who else he might turn to; only Batos came to mind.

Since Mark would not help him, Batos was the only option.

But Lawrence remembered that when Batos tipped him off about Amati's plan, he'd said the boy's plan was not exactly praiseworthy.

Batos hauled ore through dangerous mountain passes — he would no doubt consider the quick buying and selling of pyrite to be rather odious.

He doubted that Batos would help him, but Lawrence had no choice but to put aside his misgivings and ask nonetheless.

Lawrence steeled himself and looked up.

It was just then that Mark spoke again. "So even the ever-composed Lawrence gets like this sometimes, eh?"

Mark's face was neither upset nor amused; he simply seemed surprised.

"Ah, apologies," Mark continued. "Don't be angry. It just seems unusual," he said, hurriedly explaining. Lawrence was also surprised at his own behavior and far from angry.

"I can't say I'm surprised with your companion being who she is and all. But you needn't go to all this effort to stop Amati, do you? Surely she won't leave you so easily. I thought as much the first time I saw her at your side. Have more confidence, man!"

Mark finally smiled, but Lawrence was expressionless as he replied, "She gave me a signed marriage certificate. The other party is Amati naturally."

Mark's eyes widened, and he realized that he'd said the wrong thing. He scratched his beard awkwardly.

Lawrence saw this and slackened his shoulders. "If nothing had happened, sure, I'd have more confidence. But something *did* happen."

"So it happened after you came by here? We never know what lies even a step ahead in life, do we? But you still have hope, so you're still running — I see."

Lawrence nodded, and Mark stuck out his lower lip and sighed.

"Still," said Mark, "I knew she was a person to be reckoned with, but I can't believe she'd be so bold…Anyway, do you have any other leads?"

"I expect I'll go talk to Mr. Batos next."

"Batos, eh? Ah, so you're going to have him talk to the *woman* for you," murmured Mark.

"...The woman?" asked Lawrence in reply.

"Huh? Oh, so you're not going to have him talk to her for you? The chronicler, I mean. You met her, right?"

"If you mean Miss Diana, I've met her, but I don't see what she has to do with this."

"So long as you're not worried about the consequences, you might try dealing with her."

"Look, what are you talking about?" asked Lawrence.

Mark looked over his shoulder conspiratorially, then lowering his voice, he spoke. "She practically coordinates the northern regions. Especially the alchemists — you might as well call her their storefront. It's because of her that the alchemists that have managed to escape persecution gather here, from our perspective. Of course, only the local nobility and elders of the town council know the details. Oh, and —"

Mark took a sip of ale and continued, "Everybody knows that the alchemists have pyrite, but nobody wants to make waves, so they don't do business with alchemists. In old Batos's case, he deals mostly with the alchemists and rarely with anybody else. No — it's more accurate to say he *can't* deal with anyone else *because* he deals with alchemists. So if you can risk the trouble it might bring, getting Batos to talk to the woman for you is an option."

It wasn't clear to Lawrence whether this sudden revelation was the truth, but Mark had nothing to gain from lying.

"Depending on the circumstances, it might be worth trying. The flames are getting quite close, after all, are they not?"

It was pathetic, but Lawrence had to admit that with Mark's refusal to help, the situation was quite desperate.

"I'm actually quite pleased that you'd turn to me for help, but this is all I can do for you," said Mark.

"No, I appreciate it. I nearly overlooked a huge opportunity."

Even Lawrence felt that Mark's reason for refusing him was completely justified.

Mark was a town merchant, and Lawrence was a traveling merchant. The abilities and limitations of each were naturally very different.

"I know I refused you...but I'll be praying for your success nonetheless."

Now it was Lawrence's turn to smile. "You've taught me something valuable. That alone was worth my time," he said with complete sincerity. In the future, when he dealt with town merchants, Lawrence would have today's experience to draw upon. It was indeed something valuable.

Whether or not it was in response to Lawrence's words, Mark stroked his beard noisily.

He frowned and looked off to the side as he spoke. "I may not be able to help you directly, but I might be able to whisper the condition of someone's wallet in your ear."

Lawrence was visibly surprised, at which Mark closed his eyes.

"Come by the shop later. I can at least tell you who to buy from."

"...Thank you, truly," said Lawrence with complete honesty.

Mark shook his head as if at a loss, sighing. "When you make that face, I guess I see why that girl would be so bold."

"...What do you mean?"

"Ah, nothing. Just that merchants should stick to business."

Lawrence wanted the laughing Mark to explain himself, but he was already focusing on Batos and Diana.

"Good luck to you," said Mark.

"Thanks."

Lawrence's chest was still tight with anxiety, and if he was to go negotiate, the sooner he did so the better.

He thanked Mark again and put Mark's stall behind him.

It was often said that the traveling merchant has no friends. As he walked the streets, Lawrence decided this was not true.

Lawrence first headed directly to the trade guild.

He had two goals: first, to discover whether Batos had a stock of pyrite on hand or any connections to buy some, and second, to have Batos take him to Diana.

He remembered Batos's dismissal of Amati's plan to raise money — not entirely praiseworthy, Batos had said.

The man hauled ore and precious stones from the mines over dangerous mountain paths. He might well find this pyrite-speculation business downright shameful.

Even though he knew he might be asking the impossible, Lawrence still had to go.

He made his way through the back alleys to the guild house, turning a blind eye to the festival, which was even at this late hour continuing with an atmosphere that was near riotous.

He finally arrived at his destination — a street lined with trade companies. Each company had lit lanterns, and there were circles of people dancing about here and there. Now and then, Lawrence caught sight of employees continuing the festivities by holding clumsy mock sword battles.

Pushing his way through the congested street, Lawrence approached the Rowen Trade Guild building. He silently slipped through the open doors and passed the guild members that were drinking and carrying on there.

The delineation between those who wanted to quietly drink inside and those who wished to join in the clamor outside seemed quite clear. Beneath the glow of the distinctive-smelling fish oil lamps, the guild hall was filled with quiet conversation and pleasant laughter.

A few seemed to notice Lawrence's arrival and looked at him curiously, but the greater part were wholly concerned with enjoying themselves.

Lawrence spied the man he was looking for among those gathered and walked straight toward him.

The man sat at a table with several other older merchants. Beneath the dim lamplight, he looked somehow hermitlike.

It was Gi Batos.

"I apologize for interrupting in the middle of your celebration," said Lawrence quietly. The older merchants with their decades of experience immediately understood that he was here for business.

They sipped their wine wordlessly, glancing at Batos.

Batos smiled briefly. "Ho there, Mr. Lawrence. What can I do for you?"

"I'm sorry this is so sudden, but I need to speak with you."

"Business, is it?"

After a short hesitation, Lawrence nodded.

"We'll talk over there. We can't let these old codgers steal all our profit, after all."

The other merchants at the table laughed, raising their cups as if to say, "We'll keep on without you."

Lawrence gave a quick bow and then followed Batos, who was heading farther into the guild house.

Standing in sharp contrast to the lively lobby, the halls of the guild house were like back alleys; the lamplight soon failed to reach them, and the clamor from those gathered faded like a fire burning on a river's distant shore.

Batos then stopped and turned. "So what is it you want to speak about?"

There was no point in beating around the bush. Lawrence spoke

177

simply and to the point. "I'm trying to lay in pyrite. I'm looking for someone with a stockpile, and I thought you might have some idea of where to start."

"Pyrite?"

"Yes."

Batos's eyes were a dark blue that bordered on black. They looked gray in the faint yellow light of the lamp.

Those eyes looked evenly at Lawrence.

"Have you any leads?" Lawrence asked again.

Batos sighed and rubbed his eyes. "Mr. Lawrence, you —"

"Yes?"

"Do you remember what I said when I told you about what the young Amati was planning?"

Lawrence nodded immediately. Of course, he remembered. "Not only that, I remember that Miss Diana hates business discussions."

Batos took his hand from his eyes and then stopped, his gaze now for the first time what one would expect from a merchant.

It was the look of a man whose life was devoted to the safe transport of goods through incredible hardship, unconcerned about how much profit would be made.

Those eyes seemed somehow wolflike.

"So you're eyeing the alchemists' stock, are you?"

"That will make this conversation easy — yes. However, I've heard that without Miss Diana's permission, no business can be had. That is why I've come to you."

Lawrence suddenly remembered when he was just starting out as a merchant — with no connections, he would visit without notice and say whatever it took to increase his business.

Batos's eyes widened slightly in surprise before he forced them back to their usual expression. "Is pyrite so lucrative that knowing all this, you still wish to deal with them?"

"No, that is not it."

"Then...you want to know your fortune or ward away illness as pyrite is rumored to do?" Batos smiled indulgently, as though he were playing with a grandchild. It was his way of poking fun.

Lawrence was neither angry nor impatient.

If it was for his own gain, a merchant could stare at a swinging scale all night, if that's what it took. "I am acting in my own interest. That I will not deny."

Batos stared wide-eyed, unmoving.

If he was turned away here, his best chance of finding a stockpile of pyrite would be gone.

Lawrence did not have the luxury of allowing that to happen.

"But I'm not after it because I'm trying to gain from the pyrite bubble. My aim is more...more basic."

Batos did not interrupt him, and Lawrence took this as his cue to continue.

"Mr. Batos, you're a traveling merchant, so surely you've had times when the goods you're hauling fall into a crevasse."

Still silence.

"When our wagon sinks in a mire, we weigh the difficulty of saving it against abandoning it to the mud. The value of the goods, the gain, the amount of cash on hand, the cost of getting assistance — the danger of being attacked by brigands even — we weigh it all and decide to abandon the cargo or not to."

Batos spoke slowly. "And you've found yourself thus, have you?"

"I have."

Batos's keen eyes seemed as though they could see to the end of a dark road.

He'd traveled the same road for a lifetime and came to Diana to hear tales of the roads he hadn't taken.

Those eyes would surely see through any lie.

But Lawrence did not waver.

For he was telling no lies.

"I am determined not to abandon my load. So long as I can get it back on my cart, I am willing to risk a bit of trouble."

Batos had to realize what the "cargo" was and why Lawrence was so desperate.

But the old merchant just closed his eyes, saying nothing.

Was there something more to say? Lawrence wondered. Should he push further?

The laughter that echoed from the lobby sounded derisive and mocking.

Precious time was slipping away.

Lawrence readied himself to speak.

And at the last possible moment, he stopped himself.

He remembered his master telling him that waiting was the most powerful weapon when asking another's favor.

"That's what I wanted to see," said Batos at that moment with a little smile. "It's a good merchant that can wait, even if time is short, when that's the only option left to him."

Lawrence realized he had been tested; cold sweat ran down his back, making him shiver.

"Of course, I was even pushier back in the old days."

"Er…"

"Ah, yes. I've no supply of pyrite, sad to say. But surely the alchemists do."

"So, then—"

Batos nodded slightly. "All you need say is 'I've come to buy a box of white feathers.' That should get you in the door. The rest is up to you. You'll have to be quite clever with dear Diana. I doubt anyone has gone to buy pyrite there yet."

"Thank you very much. By way of thanks—"

"As long as you'll tell me a good tale, I'll call it even. What do you think? Do I sound as dignified as Diana?"

Batos grinned childishly; Lawrence couldn't help but laugh.

Batos continued, "You never know when she's sleeping, Diana, so you should be able to go over there right now. And if you're going, you should go soon. Time is money and all." He pointed to the back of the trade guild. "If you take the back way, you can leave without answering any questions."

Lawrence thanked Batos and headed down the hall. He looked back to see the old merchant still smiling.

There with his back to the lamplight from the lobby, Batos looked a bit like his old master, Lawrence thought.

Leaving the guild house and heading north, Lawrence soon ran right into the stone wall.

He hadn't been lucky enough to arrive at the entrance, so he ran along the wall for a while until he found it, levering the rickety door open and slipping inside.

There were, of course, no lights, but as Lawrence ran, his eyes adjusted to the gloom, and as a traveling merchant who camped on the road quite a bit, he was used to a bit of darkness.

However, the slivers of light that sliced out from between the cracks in the district's wooden doors, the meowing of cats in the distance, and the sudden occasional beating of birds' wings were all much more unsettling than they had been during the day.

Without the keen sense of direction common among traveling merchants, Lawrence might have become lost and wound up sprinting away in fear.

When he finally found Diana's house, his relief was genuine.

It was like he'd arrived at a friendly woodcutter's cabin after a long walk through an ominous forest.

But on the other side of the door, which Lawrence stood in front of, there was perhaps not a friend who'd welcome him with open arms.

Even though he'd gotten the password from Batos, when Lawrence thought back on his exchange with Diana, he felt she truly did hate business.

He wondered if he would really be able to buy any pyrite.

The uncertainty grew in his chest, but he took a deep breath and pushed it back down.

He *had* to obtain the mineral.

"Excuse me, is anyone home?" Lawrence asked hesitantly, knocking lightly on the door.

The silence of someone home but asleep is subtly different from the silence of no one being present.

When it is the former, it was somehow hard to raise one's voice.

There was no reaction from behind the door.

A bit of light shone through the cracks, though, so even if Diana might have been asleep, she seemed to be there.

The town leveled harsh punishments at those who left their lamps burning as they slept, but it was hard to imagine the evening patrols venturing into this district.

Just as Lawrence was about to knock on the door again, he heard someone move behind it.

"Who is it?" The voice sounded sleepy, weary.

"I apologize for disturbing you at this late hour. I am Lawrence; I visited you yesterday with Mr. Batos."

A short pause followed, after which he heard the rustling of fabric. Next, the door slowly opened.

Light poured out of the house, along with the air from within the room.

Diana's eyes were annoyed and sleepy.

She wore the same style of robe she'd had on when he visited her before. Being a former nun, she probably wore that style year-round, morning and night, making it impossible for Lawrence to tell from her dress whether he'd woken her.

In any case, it was extremely rude to visit a woman living alone in the middle of the night; Lawrence knew this but spoke without hesitation.

"I know it's very rude, but I had to come." He continued, "I wish to buy a box of white feathers."

Diana's eyes narrowed for a moment upon hearing the password that Batos had told Lawrence. She moved aside and wordlessly gestured for him to come inside.

The inside of her house — which was free from the stench of sulfur — seemed to be even more cluttered than it had been the previous day.

Even the room's sole trace of organization — the bookshelves — were a mess, with most of the books now off the shelves, left open with their pages staring up at the ceiling.

And there were even more white quill pens scattered about than before.

"My goodness, so many guests all on the same day. The festival really does bring people out," said Diana, mostly to herself. She sat — and as before, she did not offer Lawrence a chair.

Lawrence was about to sit anyway in one of the chairs not piled high with things, but then he realized something.

So many guests.

So people had come before Lawrence.

"I expect it was Mr. Batos that told you to ask for a box of white feathers?"

Lawrence was still worried about who had come calling here, but he shook his head to clear it. "Ah, yes. I'm sorry to say I forced the issue and made him tell me how to meet with you..."

"Goodness, really? I have a hard time imagining anyone *forcing* Batos to do anything," said Diana with an amused smile.

Lawrence had nothing to say to that.

Her personality was different, but something about Diana reminded Lawrence distinctly of Holo.

"So what business is it that's so pressing you managed to convince that stubborn old coot?"

There were any number of people who would desire the skills and products alchemists possessed for a variety of reasons.

Diana was a dam that held those desires in check.

Lawrence did not know why, but Diana — sitting in her chair and looking evenly at him — seemed somehow like a great bird, guarding her eggs with iron wings.

"I need to purchase pyrite," said Lawrence, despite being half-overwhelmed by Diana's mien.

Diana put one white hand to her cheek. "I hear the price has gotten quite high."

"That's not —"

"Of course, dear Mr. Batos would never have helped you over something as simple as mere profit. So there must be some other reason, no?"

He felt like Diana was always one step ahead of him. She was quicker than Lawrence and seemed fully willing to demonstrate that.

Mustn't get angry, Lawrence told himself. He was being tested.

He nodded. "It's not business. I need pyrite for a battle."

Diana's eyes narrowed as she smiled. "A battle with whom?"

"It's…"

He hesitated to mention Amati's name. It wasn't because he thought it would be inappropriate.

It was because he wondered whether Amati was his true opponent in this battle.

He shook his head. "No, it's —" Lawrence looked back to Diana. "It's against my cargo."

"Cargo?"

"A traveling merchant's enemy is always his cargo. Estimating its value, planning for its transport, deciding upon its destination. If he errs in even one of these, he will lose. At this very moment, I am trying to recover a piece that has fallen from my wagon. Having reevaluated the value, the transport, and the destination, I have realized that this is a piece of cargo I cannot afford to lose."

Diana's bangs fluttered in what seemed like the breeze — but no, it was her own breath as she exhaled.

She smiled softly and retrieved a quill pen that was at her feet.

"'Buying a box of white feathers' is nothing more than a glorified password. All it means is that I don't mind so long as I'm able to have a bit of fun. Does a bird not drop feathers when it beats its wings excitedly? Those people that I give my password to help me choose my visitors carefully, so all I need to do is glance at them to tell. I don't mind a bit as far as pyrite goes. Buy it up as you please."

Lawrence jumped to his feet. "Thank —"

"However," said Diana, cutting him off. Lawrence suddenly had a very bad feeling.

Several visitors in a single day. A chair with nothing piled on it.

It can't be — the black words floated up in Lawrence's mind.

Diana's face was now apologetic. "Someone has already come to buy."

It was just as he'd feared.

He immediately asked the questions any merchant would ask.

"How much did they buy? What did it sell at?"

185

"Do calm yourself. The customer in question bought on credit and did not leave with the pyrite. You could say they simply made an order. For my part, I wouldn't mind letting you have the material instead. Let us try to negotiate with the first party, shall we? As for the amount, I seem to recall it being sixteen thousand *irehd* worth at current market value."

That was four hundred *trenni*. If he could acquire that much, it would be a giant boon to his plans. "I understand. Might you tell me who the buyer was...?"

If Diana were to say it was Amati, Lawrence's hopes would be obliterated.

But she only shook her head slightly. "I will handle the negotiation. For safety's sake, we do not allow others to know the identity of those who have dealt with us alchemists."

"B-but—"

"You have an objection?" She smiled coldly.

Lawrence was the one asking the favor; he could only remain silent.

"You've said this is a battle, so I presume the circumstances are not ordinary. I will help all I can and let you know the results as soon as possible. Where will I be able to find you tomorrow?"

"Ah, er...the marketplace in front of the stone seller's booth. I'll be there the entire time the market is open. Otherwise, if you contact Mark the wheat seller, his stand is..."

"I know the place. I'll send a messenger as soon as I'm able."

"Thank you." Lawrence couldn't think of anything else to say.

Yet the fact was that depending on the results of Diana's negotiation, it was still possible that he would be unable to buy any pyrite. The consequences would be near fatal.

There was only so much he could say.

"I won't hesitate to pay a considerable sum. I can't pay double market value or anything like that, but please inform them I will be quite generous."

Diana smiled and nodded, standing up from her chair.

Lawrence realized it was time for him to take his leave. The fact that he hadn't been turned away after showing up uninvited at this ridiculous hour was enough of a miracle already.

"I do apologize for calling so suddenly at this hour."

"Not at all. Night and day are meaningless to me."

Somehow he knew she wasn't joking, and yet he laughed anyway.

"And so long as you've brought interesting stories, you could stay all night and I wouldn't mind a bit."

Her words could have been interpreted as seduction, but Lawrence knew she was just being sincere.

Unfortunately, he'd already told her the one interesting story he knew.

In its place, a question appeared unbidden in his mind.

"Is something wrong?" asked Diana.

Lawrence was stopped in his tracks by the thought that struck him.

Flustered, he claimed it was nothing before heading for the door.

The question was preposterous. He couldn't possibly ask it.

"Being so mysterious when you leave a woman's home — honestly, you'll be lucky if the gods don't punish you," said Diana girlishly. Her playful smile made him think that she really would answer whatever question he cared to ask.

And she was probably the only one who could.

He turned to speak even as he reached for the door.

"I...have a question."

"Ask whatever you like," she said without hesitating.

Lawrence cleared his throat. "Are there any stories of gods... and humans, that is...falling in love, becoming a pair?"

He knew he wouldn't be able to answer if Diana asked why he wanted to know this.

Yet despite the risks, Lawrence had to ask.

Holo had wept, saying if she had a child, she would no longer be alone.

If this was at all possible, he wanted to tell her and perhaps give her some small hope.

Diana was stunned for a moment by this question, but she soon regained her composure and answered in a slow and measured voice.

"There are many."

"Really?" said Lawrence in spite of himself.

"Yes, for example — ah, but I'm sorry. You were in a hurry."

"Ah, er, yes. But perhaps later... if you wouldn't mind, I would very much like to hear the details."

"Certainly."

Fortunately, she did not ask his reasons for wanting to know.

Lawrence thanked her profusely and made ready to leave Diana's house.

Just as he was closing the door, he thought he heard her say something very softly: "Good luck to you."

When he turned to ask, the door was already closed.

Did she know of the battle between him and Amati?

Something was strange about the conversation, but Lawrence had no time to dwell on it.

Next, he needed to return to Mark's stall and then search out others who might possess pyrite in quantity.

He was short on time — and as if that wasn't bad enough, he had essentially no pyrite on hand.

Were this to continue, it would be no contest at all. His only recourse would be to pray for divine intervention.

Even if it meant leaning on his friend, Lawrence had to get

Mark to give him some names, and even if he had to pay more than it was worth, he had to get pyrite.

Lawrence wondered to himself if his frantic nocturnal dealings would bring him any closer to Holo, and his only answer was uncertainty.

When he arrived back at Mark's stall, Lawrence found Mark sitting at the same table, still drinking ale, though now his apprentice was beside him, devouring a piece of bread.

Just as Lawrence thought it an odd time for the boy to be taking dinner, Mark noticed his presence.

"Any luck?" he asked.

"Just what you see," said Lawrence, waving his hands lightly as he looked Mark in the eye. "I spoke with Diana, but someone's beaten me to it. No telling how this'll turn out."

"Someone got there first?"

"I've no choice but to place my hopes in what you told me."

Given Diana's willingness to cooperate, Lawrence guessed the odds were maybe 70–30 of that working out.

But he expected that acting like there was no hope would make Mark a bit more sympathetic.

In his previous exchange with Mark, Lawrence had learned that his request for aid was an unreasonable one from the perspective of a town merchant.

Which left an appeal to emotion as the only other option.

However, Mark's reply was slow in coming.

"Ah . . . yes, about that."

Lawrence listened to the noncommittal statement as the blood drained from his face.

Mark thwacked his apprentice on the head, gesturing with his chin. "So? Let's hear the results."

The boy gulped down a bite of bread and quickly stood up out

of the log chair. "If we pay in *trenni* silver, then … three hundred seventy pieces' worth of py —"

"Don't just say it in front of everyone!" Mark looked around hastily as he clamped a thick hand over the boy's mouth. If the conversation were overheard, it would be trouble. "So that's how it is."

Lawrence was confused.

Paying in *trenni* silver? Three hundred seventy pieces' worth?

"Ha-ha, I can't help but enjoy it when you make that face. See, after you left, I thought it over."

Mark took his hand from the boy's mouth and reached for his ale cup, his tone amused.

"I refused your request because I have a reputation to uphold. Any other town merchant would do the same. But even I have bought some you-know-what to make some money on the side — and many others have done likewise. The reason I can only buy a limited amount is that I have very little cash on hand. By all rights, the price of wheat should be dropping since the people laying in goods for their return trips haven't been buying wheat. And yet the people who've come to sell wheat are selling it right off — which is where all my cash has gone. So …"

Mark gulped down some ale, belching comfortably before continuing.

"So what of the people who *do* have cash? I can't believe they'd be able to resist. They've probably been buying up you-know-what in large quantities behind the scenes. And here's where you need some backstory. You see, these merchants aren't lone wolves like you. Each one has their business, their position, their reputation. And they've bought this stuff, but the price has risen so high that it's getting hard to sell. All they need do is sell a little bit to bring in a surprising profit, but this makes some of them even more nervous. So what happens next? I'm sure a clever fellow like you can figure it out."

Lawrence nodded his head after a moment.

Mark must have had his apprentice running all over town, spreading a rumor — a rumor that had to go something like this: There's a mad traveling merchant in town who wants to buy pyrite with cash. Why not take the chance to unload some of that pyrite that's not selling?

It would be a perfect opportunity for those merchants.

And to be sure, there was no question that Mark had signed a contract promising him a service fee for brokering the hidden transaction.

It was brilliant — conducting a pyrite deal under the pretense of doing someone a favor.

But to have been able to pull together 370 *trenni* worth — there was clearly pressure to sell in the marketplace.

"So that's how it is. If you're on board, I'll send the boy out immediately."

There was no reason to refuse.

Lawrence undid the tie of the burlap sack he had on his back.

But then he stopped. "Still —"

Mark regarded him dubiously.

Lawrence returned to himself and quickly retrieved a bag of silver coins from the sack and placed it on the table. "Sorry," he muttered.

Mark seemed momentarily at a loss for Lawrence's strange behavior. "This is when you thank me, right?"

"Ah, er, yes, sor...no, I mean —" Lawrence suddenly felt like he was speaking to Holo. "I mean, thanks."

"Bwa-ha-ha-ha! If I'd known you were such an amusing guy, I'd have...Actually, I suppose not."

Mark took the bag of silver from Lawrence and quickly looked at it; then he undid the string and handed the bag to his apprentice, who quickly emptied its contents and began counting the silver pieces.

"You've changed," said Mark.

"...Is that so?"

"Quite. You used to be not an excellent merchant, but a merchant *wholly* from head to toe. That's all there was of you. You never even truly thought of me as a friend, did you?"

Mark had the right of it. Lawrence had no response.

The wheat seller just smiled, though. "But what of now? Am I merely a convenient merchant to do a deal with?"

Lawrence was momentarily stunned. He couldn't possibly nod at this statement.

Feeling as though he were trapped in the center of some strange illusion, he shook his head no.

"That's why I could never content myself with the life of a traveling merchant. But there's something even more interesting."

Was this because Mark had been drinking? Or was there some other reason?

Mark continued, sounding truly amused. His face was chestnut round now despite the square cut of his beard.

"Let me ask you one thing. If it were me whose separation you were faced with, would you be running around town as frantically as you are now?"

The boy, who lived every day with Mark as his master, looked up at the two men.

Lawrence found this all very mysterious.

Though he certainly thought of Mark as a friend, he could not honestly bring himself to nod and say "yes" to that question.

"Ha-ha-ha-ha. Well, I look forward to the future. Still"— he paused, then continued quietly — "it's for your companion that you're so desperate."

Lawrence felt as though he'd swallowed something hot and felt it pass down into his stomach.

Mark looked at his apprentice. "This is what a man looks like when he's obsessed with a woman. But it's the unbending branch that breaks in a strong wind."

A single year weathered alone was worth less than half a year with company.

So how much older than Lawrence might Mark be?

"You're no different from me. You've got the traveling merchant's curse," said Mark.

"C-curse?"

"But it's almost broken, which is what's made you so amusing. Do you not see? Did you not begin traveling with your current companion out of nothing more than good fortune?"

Holo had happened to hide herself in his wheat-filled wagon as Lawrence had passed through the village.

That he'd become close to her was nothing more or less than good fortune's gift.

"Bwa-ha-ha! I feel like I'm looking at myself when I first met Adele! You've got the curse, all right."

Lawrence felt like he finally understood.

Though Holo was very important to him, there was a part of him that always preserved a certain cool distance between them.

He hadn't realized how blind he'd become to his surroundings because of Holo.

It was an unbalancing situation.

"The curse...You mean that famous 'traveling merchant's complaint'?"

Mark guffawed, then smacked his apprentice — who'd stopped working — upside the head. "The poets will tell you that money can't buy love, and the priest will tell you that there are things more precious than money. But if that's so, why is it we labor so hard to earn money, then gain something even more precious?"

Lawrence had thought so little about what exactly Holo *was* to him because she was always right there beside him.

If her presence had been something he had gained only after laboring long and hard, he would not have been so ambivalent.

He'd always believed that anything truly precious required much effort to gain.

If she was to ask him "What am I to you?" now, Lawrence was sure he could answer.

"Ah, such a fine tale I've not told in a long time. Combined with the information on conditions in the north, why, ten *lumione* seems a bargain!"

"If you'd made all this up, it'd be extortion," said Lawrence indignantly. Mark only grinned, which in turn teased a smile out of Lawrence.

"I hope all goes well for you."

Lawrence nodded, his mood clear like a cloudless evening sky.

"Though I suppose how it turns out is up to you…"

"Hm?"

"Ah, nothing," said Mark with a shake of his head. He gestured to the boy, who had finished counting up the silver coins. The apprentice was a model of competence as he made his preparations and was ready to depart a moment later.

"Right, off with you, then." Mark sent the apprentice on his way and then turned back to Lawrence. "So where will you be sleeping tonight?"

"Haven't decided yet."

"Well, then —"

"Wait, I've decided. May I sleep here?"

Mark gave Lawrence a blank look. "Here?"

"Quite — you've wheat sacks aplenty. Lend me a few of those."

"I can certainly lend you some, but come to my house. I won't even charge you."

"Ah, but this will bring luck." The practice was something many a traveling merchant believed.

Mark gave up on pressing his invitation further. "I'll see you here, dawn tomorrow."

Lawrence nodded, and Mark raised his cup.

"A toast then to your dreams."

Lawrence found he had no reason to refuse.

CHAPTER FIVE

Lawrence sneezed grandly.

Of course, it didn't make a difference when he traveled alone, but lately he'd had a certain cheeky, irritable companion, so Lawrence always minded himself. Now, though, it seemed he was slipping — hence the sneeze.

He frantically checked to see if the other occupant of the blanket was still asleep — only to realize that side was rather cold.

And then he remembered that he was alone, sleeping on the wheat sacks next to Mark's stall.

" . . . "

He'd tried to prepare himself for it and had after all chosen to sleep alone, but upon awakening, he still felt a huge sense of loss.

Lawrence was used to someone being beside him when he awoke.

He had become so quickly accustomed to it that only now did he realize its value.

Lawrence overcame his reluctance to part from his warm blanket and stood up suddenly.

Frigid air immediately attacked him.

The morning sky was still dim, but already Mark's apprentice was sweeping the area in front of the stall.

"Oh, good morning, sir."

"Good morning," said Lawrence.

It didn't seem like this was a show put on for the benefit of his master's acquaintance; undoubtedly it was the boy's habit to wake this early in order to prepare the stall for opening. He casually greeted a few other boys that passed by.

He was an admirable apprentice.

More than whatever training Mark had given him, the boy simply seemed like an excellent individual.

"Ah, that reminds me —"

The boy turned around smartly as soon as Lawrence spoke.

"Did you hear from Mark what's happening today?"

"Er, no...are we not forcing the dastardly villain into a trap?" asked the apprentice.

The boy lowered his voice and spoke in such an exaggeratedly serious fashion that Lawrence was stunned for a moment. With a true merchant's discipline, he managed to keep a straight face and nodded. "I can't tell you all the details, but that's it, more or less. I may have to ask a serious favor of you in the process."

The boy held his broom at his side like a sword and gulped.

Seeing the boy made Lawrence sure of one thing.

He might well have been the promising young apprentice of a wheat seller, but in his heart he still longed for the life of a knight.

After all, one only sees "dastardly villains" in fairy tales.

Lawrence got a ticklish feeling, as though he was looking back on his younger self.

"What's your name, lad?"

"Ah, er, it's —"

When a merchant asked another person for their name, it was an acknowledgment of that person's status.

The boy had probably never been asked his name before in his life.

Despite his visible fluster, he really was an admirable lad, Lawrence felt.

The boy straightened up and answered. "Landt. My name is Eu Landt."

"Born in the northlands, were you?"

"Yes, from a village frozen in snow and frost."

Lawrence saw that Landt's description was not just an easy way to convey a sense of his hometown, but a literal description of how it must have seemed when he looked back on it for the last time.

That was how things were in the north.

"I see. Well, I'm counting on you today, Landt." Lawrence extended his right hand, and Landt hurried to wipe his own hand off on his tunic before shaking Lawrence's proffered hand.

The boy's palm was rough and callused, and who knew what sort of future it might grasp?

Lawrence knew he had to win.

He let the boy's hand go.

"Well then, first let's fill our bellies, eh? Is there anyplace nearby that's selling food yet?"

"There's a stand that sells dry bread to travelers. Shall I go and buy some?"

"Indeed," said Lawrence and produced two tarnished *irehd* pieces that were so dark they looked almost coppery.

"Er, one piece should be plenty," said Landt.

"The other's an advance on your help today. Of course, I'll pay you a proper consideration when it's all done."

The boy was stunned.

Smiling, Lawrence added, "If you dawdle, Mark's liable to arrive. No doubt he'll claim breakfast is a luxury, don't you think?"

Landt nodded hastily and then dashed off.

Lawrence watched his form recede for a while, and then he

turned his gaze to the spaces between the many stalls across the street.

"Don't you spoil my apprentice now."

"You could've stopped me."

Mark's form appeared in the space between crates. His expression seemed irritable, and he sighed. "It's gotten cold lately. If he takes ill because I haven't let him eat enough, that's more trouble for me."

It was clear enough that Mark had a good deal of affection for Landt.

But having Landt get some breakfast was no simple act of kindness; it was an important part of Lawrence's plan.

Merchants were not saints, after all. Whatever their actions, they always have ulterior motives.

"Should be good weather today," said Mark. "Good for selling," he finished with a nod.

Lawrence took a deep breath.

The bracing morning air felt good.

When he exhaled, all the unnecessary thoughts in his mind seemed to leave with his breath.

All he had to think about now was making his plan succeed.

Once success was his, he could second-guess and doubt all he wanted.

"Right then, time to fill my stomach," said Lawrence heartily as he caught sight of a winded Landt returning.

The atmosphere itself was different.

That was the first thing that struck Lawrence as he arrived at the marketplace.

What at first look seemed to be as quiet as a glassy lake's surface was a roiling boil as soon as one touched it.

Ever since sunrise, a single corner of the marketplace was the focus of an unusually dense crowd, and every person's gaze was turned to a single stall.

It was the sole stone seller in the town of Kumersun, and the only detail the crowd cared about was a makeshift board with prices written on it.

On the price board were written descriptions of the weight and shape of pieces of pyrite, and beside each description line was a wooden placard with the price and the number of people in line to buy it.

There was another column on the board that listed sellers, but it seemed unlikely that there would be a chance for these placards to stay there for long.

The board made obvious the supply and demand for pyrite, and the demand was high.

"Looks like the average price is…eight hundred *irehd*."

That was eighty times the old price.

It could only be described as absurd. Like a runaway horse with no rider to check it, the price kept rising and rising.

Presented with an opportunity for easy money, human reason was like reins of mud—completely incapable of stopping this runaway horse.

Though the market bell would not ring for some time, there seemed to be a tacit approval for doing early deals. Once Lawrence reached that stand, he caught sight of merchants approaching the master occasionally to whisper a few words. Once a number of deals had been reached, the master would quietly replace the relevant wooden placards.

The master didn't update the prices and line numbers immediately, probably to keep others from knowing exactly who had purchased pyrite and at what price.

But in any case, the number of people waiting to buy kept rising.

Just as Lawrence was estimating the total amount being spent, a figure appeared at the edge of his vision.

He looked. It was Amati.

Lawrence had seen Amati before Amati had spotted him the previous night, but the young merchant was sharp-eyed enough not to let chances for profit escape. His gaze was every bit as keen as Lawrence's, and he soon caught sight of his rival.

A friendly greeting would hardly have been appropriate.

But since Lawrence had arranged to collect the cash he was owed upon the sounding of the bell that opened the marketplace, he could hardly ignore Amati, either.

Just as he considered this, Amati revealed a smile and nodded slightly.

Lawrence was taken aback for a moment but soon understood the reason.

Beside Amati was Holo.

For whatever reason, she was not dressed as a town girl, but instead wore her nun's robes. Three pure white feathers, vivid enough to be visible at a distance, were affixed to her hood.

She looked steadily at the stone seller's stall, not once meeting Lawrence's eye.

Heat rose in his belly at Amati's smile.

Holo whispered something in Amati's ear before the the young merchant made his way through the gathered merchants toward Lawrence, and Lawrence feigned total serenity, as if the anger he felt did not exist.

He had confidence that as long as he did not have to fool Holo, his charade would go unchallenged.

"Good morning, Mr. Lawrence."

"And to you."

It took some effort for Lawrence to maintain his facade in the face of Amati's pleasant greeting.

"Things are going to become quite hectic once the bell rings, so I thought it would be best to turn this over to you ahead of time," said Amati, producing a small bag from near his breast.

In size it was more of a coin purse than anything else. "What's this?" Lawrence asked, having expected Amati to give him the agreed-upon silver coins.

The bag was far too small to carry three hundred pieces of silver.

"This is the promised amount," said Amati.

Having no other choice, Lawrence suspiciously accepted the bag.

When he opened the bag's mouth and looked inside, his eyes widened.

"It might have been a bit presumptuous of me," said Amati, "but three hundred silver pieces would be quite cumbersome, so I took the liberty of remitting in gold *limar* coins."

Though it was hard to imagine how he'd managed to obtain them, the bag was indeed filled with gold coins.

The gold *limar* was not as valuable as the *lumione*, but it was a widely circulated coin within Ploania, the country in which Kumersun was situated. It was worth about twenty *trenni*.

But managing to obtain this amount during a currency shortage — the service charge must have been incredibly steep.

The only reason to do it was for Amati to prove how much coin he had on hand — it was a psychological attack.

Amati had Holo in tow, too, probably as another way to divert Lawrence's attention.

Lawrence had inadvertently widened his eyes in surprise, so there could be no concealing his perturbation.

"I've used today's exchange rate to prepare the amount. Fourteen gold *limar*."

"...Understood. I accept."

"Do you not wish to count the coins?"

Normally saying "There's no need," as Lawrence did, should've shown confidence, but now it just seemed as though he was merely pretending at strength.

"In that case, I'd like the contract for three hundred silver."

Lawrence only did so after being asked.

Amati was still one step ahead of him.

Once the cash and the partially fulfilled contract had been exchanged, Amati was even the first to say, "Very well."

As he watched Amati's receding form, one ill realization after another flashed through Lawrence's mind.

When they had signed the contract the previous day, Amati may have claimed to have insufficient cash as an excuse to provide the horses in lieu of coin.

Always keeping a certain amount of cash on hand was a trait shared by all merchants.

What was worse, Amati had surely searched out and bought pyrite just as Lawrence had.

If Amati had gathered enough, all he would require was a very small increase in price.

Thinking back on the way Amati had just bowed so gracefully and turned around after accepting the contract, Lawrence could not believe that it had been a bluff.

Just how much pyrite had the boy managed to buy?

Lawrence feigned rubbing his nose and instead bit his thumbnail.

His original plan had been to observe carefully and then begin selling off quantities of pyrite starting at noon to check the rising price.

Suddenly Lawrence wondered if he should move more quickly.

But Diana's messenger had not arrived yet.

Until he knew whether or not he would be able to obtain the necessary amounts, Lawrence couldn't act.

He could purchase more pyrite using the gold Amati had paid

him but if Diana's negotiations on his behalf succeeded and he received another four hundred silver pieces' worth, that would also be a problem.

He'd set aside money to pay Diana with so that was not an issue, but he would have too much of the mineral.

Of course, he'd been purchasing pyrite in order to be able to force a drop in its price, and he'd been careful to buy just enough to be able to control that drop, in order to avoid his own bankruptcy.

Admittedly, if Lawrence was willing to ruin himself in order to stop Amati for Holo's sake, she might finally accept his sincerity.

Of course, the story would not end so easily — he still needed to live on something after that.

The weight of reality bore down on him heavier than the gold coins in his hand.

The stone shop's price board was updated again.

It seemed someone had just bought a large amount of pyrite; both the prices and the line numbers jumped dramatically.

How much would Amati's pyrite be worth after this jump?

Lawrence felt unable to simply stand by and do nothing.

But losing his cool could lead to defeat.

He closed his eyes, lowered the hand with the fingernails he'd been biting from his mouth, and took a deep breath.

Everything he had been thinking was all due to Amati's bluffing.

After all, behind Amati was Holo. If Lawrence could just discern everyone's ulterior motives, he would be fine.

Just then, the clear tone of a ringing bell swept overhead.

It was the signal for the market to open.

The battle had begun.

The charged atmosphere seemed to induce everyone to stay scrupulously honest and calm.

They had been waiting for some time in front of the stone seller's stand but only began to move once the bell rang.

An examination of the crown revealed travelers and farmers furtively selling small quantities of pyrite — but the small-scale selling only served to further heat the marketplace.

In a situation where none were willing to sell, the only people with an advantage were those who already had a large stock of pyrite — it was thanks to the small-scale selling along with new buyers that kept people excited and close to the stall's front.

Since each person there thought they had a chance to profit, none left.

Given such an environment, it would take a serious amount of pyrite in order to force the price down — nothing less would do.

The price board, which occasionally disappeared behind the heads of the people in the crowd, was a thermometer for the marketplace, and it was constantly rising.

Diana's messenger still had not arrived.

If her negotiations failed, he would have to take action quickly.

The thoughts pained him as he stared at the price board, and suddenly Amati appeared in his field of vision in front of the stall.

Panic washed over Lawrence, and he wanted to dash forward, clutching the bag of what pyrite he had to his breast.

But if that was Amati's plan to shake him up, such a move could be disastrous. If Lawrence sold off only a middling amount, it would just increase demand as buyers assumed they would be able to purchase pyrite so long as they waited long enough, and as the line grew longer, the price would continue to rise.

Lawrence controlled his urge to sell, praying that this was a ploy on Amati's part.

Then he realized something.

Holo was gone.

Lawrence glanced around and saw that at some point Holo had

moved outside of the strange crowd of people and was looking at him.

When their eyes met, she narrowed hers in displeasure, then turned, and began to walk away.

As he saw this, sweat sprung upon Lawrence's back.

This had to be a trap that Holo was hinting at.

If she had heard of the circumstances surrounding pyrite from Amati, it was entirely possible she'd contrived a way to trap Lawrence. Someone as clever as Holo would surely notice things that Amati would miss, even if he was the one explaining the situation to her.

And Holo excelled at discerning what was in people's hearts. She was unparalleled at such times.

As soon as he thought of this, Lawrence was assaulted by a vision of the quagmire that surrounded him.

No matter where he stepped, he would sink into the mud; no matter whose movements he watched, they would be illusions.

Lawrence suspected darkly that this was all part of Holo's plan.

The terror of having a sly wolf circling him thus sunk into his body.

Yet Lawrence couldn't abandon hope that Holo was merely doing this out of some perverse obstinacy.

The poisons of assumption and doubt penetrated his mind.

He stared blankly at the price board, though this was not his intention. It was simply all he could do at the moment.

The price of pyrite continued to inch upward.

Fortunately, since the price was already so preposterously inflated, the rate of the increase was quite slow.

Still, if the price continued to increase at this rate, it would certainly reach by noon the 20 percent needed by Amati.

To Lawrence's knowledge, Amati's current stock of pyrite was worth eight hundred silver pieces. If the price rose twenty percent, he would need only forty more silver pieces to reach the required thousand.

And if all he needed was forty coins, Amati would surely be able to produce them.

He could sell whatever of his fortune he needed to and complete the contract on the spot. If that happened, the margin sale poison that Lawrence counted on would undoubtedly have little effect.

Where *was* Diana's messenger?

Lawrence muttered to himself, a consuming panic sinking into his gut.

Even if he was to start scrambling to buy pyrite now, how much would he be able to collect?

It was not like the previous night, where the market had already closed and no one knew whether the price would rise or fall next — no, now it was utterly obvious that the price was rising.

Anybody who had pyrite knew it was like free money — nobody would sell to him under such circumstances.

The realization hit him — his plan could only succeed if he got the pyrite from Diana, and at this rate, he might wind up taking a huge blow from Amati because of the margin-selling contract, as well.

Lawrence rubbed his eye and thought hard. He had planned to pursue his goal coolly and logically, but he was starting to feel as though he'd been forced into a complete dead end.

No, he told himself.

He knew what the problem was.

It was not because of the fluctuating price of pyrite.

Behind that was the fact that he now regarded Holo with despair rather than trust.

She had arrived with Amati at the marketplace — it was possible that rather than meeting up in the morning, they'd spent the night together.

Holo might have invited Amati back to the inn after Lawrence had arranged the margin-selling contract with him.

Depending on the circumstances, she might even have shown him her ears and tail and told him the truth of her existence.

Lawrence wanted to believe such a thing was impossible, but he remembered that Holo had revealed her true nature to him the same day they'd met. It was the height of folly to believe that she had somehow marked him and only him as particularly open-minded.

Amati was clearly and madly in love with Holo; no doubt she could evaluate anyone as quickly as she had Lawrence.

And what if Amati had accepted her?

He remembered the young merchant's smile only moments ago.

Holo feared being alone.

And Lawrence was not sure that she wanted to be with him and only him.

The realization that he should not be thinking this way hit him, and his legs nearly collapsed under him at the shock of it.

It was out of sheer luck that he didn't fall.

Suddenly a murmur ran through the crowd, bringing Lawrence back to himself.

He turned to look at the *oohs!* that arose, only to see that the price of the most expensive pyrite had jumped significantly.

Someone had put in a large bid.

Its acceptance meant that others would soon follow suit.

It might already be impossible to stop Amati from fulfilling the contract.

The fact that there was still no word from Diana suggested that the other party might be being stubborn; if the price of pyrite continued to rise, that would only make them more reluctant to sell.

It was looking more and more as if Lawrence should abandon that hope and take action now.

The weapons he had on hand were four hundred silver pieces' worth of pyrite, along with the rumor that Landt had been given to spread.

It was such a pathetic arsenal that Lawrence wanted to laugh. He now seriously doubted the idea he'd had such faith in the previous day, that a mere rumor could do any damage. Only yesterday it had been his secret weapon, the product of his years of experience.

It was becoming more and more clear to him just how drunk he must have been.

He realized he was already trying to think of a contingency plan.

If he did nothing, he would still receive one thousand silver pieces from Amati, which would leave him a tidy profit even after subtracting the losses from the margin selling.

Lawrence was disgusted by how much lighter this made him feel.

...*If you could receive a thousand silver coins for me, it would not be so regrettable to let me go* — Holo's accusation hit him.

Lawrence remembered the letter from Diana that was tucked near his breast.

It was the information that would help him find Holo's home of Yoitsu. Perhaps he no longer had any right to hold this letter.

I'm just a lowly merchant. Lawrence thought to himself as he looked around for Holo.

The events that happened in the port town of Pazzio and the Church city of Ruvinheigen had been but a dream.

As soon as the thought struck him, he realized that it seemed to be exactly so.

Lawrence smiled weakly as he looked into the hotly swirling crowd, but Holo was nowhere to be found, so he moved elsewhere.

Some time had passed since the opening of the market, but the day's festival had not yet started, so more and more people seemed to be making their way in.

Holo remained elusive.

Cursing his inability to find her now — *now of all times!* — he realized something.

After he'd met her gaze in the crowd, Holo had walked away.

Had she simply left right then and there?

If so, where had she gone? Had she decided his failure was a foregone conclusion, Lawrence wondered, and returned to the inn?

It would stand to reason.

The idea was so humiliating that Lawrence felt broken just thinking it — and yet he believed it himself.

He wanted some wine.

Immediately after the thought occurred to him, he uttered a small, questioning sound. "Huh?"

He'd been scanning a fairly small area, so his eyes were bound to notice the detail eventually.

Amati had entered his field of vision, which caused Lawrence to make a noise of confusion and surprise.

Amati's right hand was pressed up against his chest, probably holding a bag of coin and pyrite.

The problem was not in what he was doing, but rather the expression of concern on his face and the way that he looked here and there, searching for something — just like Lawrence.

Lawrence suspected Amati of putting on some kind of act.

But then by some miracle, the crowd between them thinned, and Amati noticed Lawrence. He was clearly surprised to see his rival.

And then Lawrence glimpsed a look of relief on Amati's face. Though the crowd quickly closed in around them and blocked Lawrence's view again, there was no mistaking what he had seen.

A single thought jumped out at Lawrence.

Amati — like him — was looking for Holo. Not only that, Amati had been relieved to see that Holo *wasn't* with Lawrence.

Lawrence felt a thump, as though someone's shoulder had bumped into him from behind.

He turned to see one mercantile-looking fellow talking excitedly with another.

That's odd, he said to himself, whereupon he felt the same thump reverberate from his back to his chest.

Then he realized.

It was the pounding of his heart.

Amati had been frantically looking for Holo and was obviously very worried that she would be with Lawrence.

The young merchant did not trust her fully.

Which in turn suggested that there was a reason for his doubt.

But what was it?

"It couldn't be —," said Lawrence.

If Amati was looking for her, that meant she had not told him where she was going.

And if that alone was enough to cause Amati stress, it was very unlikely she had revealed her ears and tail to him.

It was enough to make Lawrence want to abandon the dark, dismal conclusions he'd come to only a moment ago and turn to brighter assumptions.

He had no confidence in his ability to tell whether or not this was wishful thinking, however.

It was vexing enough to make him nauseous.

Suddenly there was another cry from the crowd.

Lawrence looked hastily toward the stone seller's stall and saw that somewhere along the line, the placard for the highest-value pyrite had been removed.

Which meant that it had sold at that price.

And that wasn't even the reason for the shouts.

The placards marking the highest values for various types of pyrite had all been taken down, and there was a drop in the number of plates for buyers in line.

Someone had sold off a considerable amount.

Lawrence fought back the nausea that rose and looked about frantically, trying to spot Amati.

He was not in front of the stall.

He wasn't even near it.

When Lawrence finally spotted him, Amati was in the crowd.

He was watching the stall with a shocked expression.

So it hadn't been Amati who had made the large sale.

Lawrence felt but a fleeting moment of relief before more placards for waiting buyers went up, along with a new round of cries from the crowd.

Nearly everyone here had at least a small amount of pyrite; they were waiting for just the right moment to buy or sell. The market was starting to fluctuate, which would become another factor for them to consider.

Essentially, now was the right time to sell.

Lawrence was on the verge of giving up — but pushing him in the opposite direction was the thought that he could still accomplish something with his plan of carefully selling off a large amount.

But he soon thought better of it, like some kind of cowardly hare.

Lawrence had no idea what Holo was thinking or where she had gone. People's hearts were not so easily understood. To think otherwise was to invite ruin.

And yet — Lawrence could not help thinking.

Expectation, suspicion, supposition, and reality were four hooks that tore at Lawrence's thoughts.

What would Holo the Wisewolf say at a time like this?

Pathetically, Lawrence couldn't help but wonder.

He felt that he could make a decision based off even her most casual observation.

He trusted her.

Just then —

"Um, excuse me —"

Lawrence felt a tug on his sleeve as the words reached his ears.

He whirled as if struck, expecting to see a certain cheeky girl behind him.

But it was a boy — Landt, to be precise.

"Um, Mr. Lawrence, may I have a moment?"

Lawrence turned with such speed that Landt was taken aback for a moment, but the boy's expression made it clear that there was urgent business.

Anxiety swept over Lawrence as he looked around; then he knelt down to bring his face closer to the much shorter Landt and nodded.

"A customer has come to our shop wishing to pay for wheat in pyrite."

Lawrence understood immediately. Mark was willing to take the offer and then sell Lawrence that pyrite, assuming Lawrence could pay cash.

"How much?"

If Mark had sent the boy all the way over here, it had to be a sizable amount.

Lawrence swallowed and waited for the reply.

"Two hundred fifty silver," said Landt.

Lawrence clenched his teeth to avoid shouting out at the unexpected development.

The wolf-god of the harvest might have abandoned him, but the goddess of fortune was still on his side.

Lawrence immediately pushed the small bag he'd gotten from Amati into Landt's hands. "Go, as fast as you can."

Landt nodded, and then tore off like an envoy carrying a vital message.

Meanwhile, the market continued to fluctuate.

Perhaps indicating that the price had topped out, the number of buyers on the line placards had changed shockingly fast.

It was clear that the buyers and sellers were beginning to turn completely against one another.

With the price this high, some would start to sell while those who needed the price to go still higher would buy.

Occasionally Lawrence would catch sight of Amati at the other side of the crowd; he had no doubt that Amati was watching him, as well.

The fact that Amati kept such a close eye on both the stone seller's stall and Lawrence suggested that he hadn't yet raised the thousand coins he needed.

No, that's not it — Lawrence corrected himself.

He might already have raised the money but was worried that if he sold off the pyrite he had on hand, trading might go awry and cause the price to crash before he could sell his entire stock.

And because Amati was party to Lawrence's margin-selling contract, a crash in price would hit him with a huge loss.

There was one other important fact, as well.

The five hundred silver pieces' worth of pyrite that Amati held still only existed in the form of a paper contract.

It could be bought or sold, yes, but the physical pyrite the contract represented could not be collected until that evening.

The market had started to fluctuate instead of simply rise, and the possibility of a drop was now much more real. If Amati was to sell the certificate, what would happen?

Margin transactions involved an interval of time between the exchange of money and goods.

In an environment where a drop in price was anticipated, a margin sale certificate — which promised future goods for immediate cash — was a joker, a worthless card with a grinning witch on it.

Once the market value of a product actually dropped, whoever held this joker would be ruined.

The slow-acting poison of Lawrence's margin sale was beginning to take effect.

Amati was still glancing this way and that, desperate.

He was obviously looking for Holo.

Holo had probably guessed what Lawrence was up to and told Amati of the trap.

The winds seemed about to change; offense and defense were reversing themselves.

If Lawrence did not strike, he would be letting a once-in-a-millennium chance go by.

People nearly attacked the stone seller's stall, and the price placards were swapped out one after another.

Lawrence held tightly to the pyrite in his breast pocket, desperately hoping Landt would return soon.

It did not take too much time to run to Mark's stall and back.

Just then —

A voice echoed across the crowd. "A purchase is in!"

Someone had been unable to contain their excitement.

In that moment, as if the market were a wave-tossed ship that had suddenly regained its stability, the mood shifted again.

Someone had purchased a large amount of pyrite. This suggested that the price would continue to rise.

Buoyed by the expectation, the crowd seemed to settle down.

Landt had yet to return.

The more time passed, the more the market seemed to steady itself.

But the number of possible buyers was dropping — Lawrence could take this opportunity to sell off a quantity of pyrite and sweep away this stability.

If he did that, he might be able to clear out the buying line even if it was just for a brief amount of time.

Doing so at this precise moment would surely have a profound effect.

Lawrence made his move.

He slipped between the crowds, pulling the bag of pyrite from his breast pocket as he arrived before the stone seller's booth.

"I'm here to sell!"

As everybody watched, Lawrence threw the bag of pyrite down in front of the stone seller.

The stone seller and his apprentices were stunned for a moment, but they quickly came to their senses and resumed business.

Lawrence had tossed a stone into a quiet lake; now came the rippling effect.

The measuring was done quickly, whereupon the apprentices that held line placards took the pyrite pieces off to the various buyers who had ordered them.

Lawrence immediately received his payment.

Without bothering to count, he grabbed the bag of coins tightly and looked back out into the crowd.

He caught a glimpse of Amati's stricken face.

Lawrence felt neither vindication nor pity.

His sole concern was his own goal.

He had sold all of the pyrite he had on hand. Any further attacks would have to wait until he had more.

Where was Landt? Where was Diana's messenger?

If he had the four hundred silver pieces' worth of pyrite he was expecting from Diana, there was no question he would be able to turn the marketplace around.

He was at the crossroads of destiny.

And then he heard a voice.

"Mr. Lawrence."

It was Landt, his forehead shiny with sweat as he ran up to Lawrence and offered him another bag.

It was 250 silver pieces' worth of pyrite.

Lawrence was torn between returning immediately to the stone seller's stall to sell the pyrite he now had on hand or waiting for Diana's messenger to come so he could be sure.

He cursed himself.

Had he not even now given up on Diana?

The negotiations had dragged on for so long. There was a limit to how optimistic Lawrence could afford to be.

He had to take his chances.

Lawrence turned and prepared to venture forth again.

There was a loud cheer that froze him in his tracks.

"Ooooh!"

The crowd blocked his view; he couldn't see what was happening.

But the instant the cheer rose, Lawrence's intuition almost compelled him to cry out and run — it told him the worst had happened.

He pushed his way back through the crowd to a place where he could see the price board.

It was admirable indeed that he didn't fall to his knees on the spot.

The top price on the board had been renewed.

Demand had pushed it back up.

It seemed some of the market buyers had decided that the disturbance a moment ago was a temporary fluctuation, and they had put in a wave of purchase orders.

Purchase line placards were put back on the board.

Lawrence suppressed the urge to vomit. The decision of whether or not to sell the pyrite he had again pressed in on him.

There was still some small chance of success if he took quick action.

No — the wise decision would be to wait for Diana's messenger.

The amount of pyrite he was negotiating for with her was worth four hundred pieces of silver then — it might well be as high as five hundred by now.

If Lawrence could add that to what he already had, it would be enough for another big sell-off.

As Lawrence was placing all his hopes in that small chance, he saw Amati, now looking much more at ease, walk away from the stall.

The young merchant was planning to sell.

It was unclear whether or not he was going to sell all he had, though.

Lawrence didn't have to know the boy's plan to realize that he would only exchange some fraction of his pyrite for coin. Amati had probably realized the nature of Lawrence's slow-acting poison, so he would want to unload the certificate first.

Why had Diana's messenger not come? Lawrence wondered if he had finally been abandoned by the gods.

In his mind, he screamed.

"Excuse me, are you Mr. Lawrence?"

In his despair, Lawrence thought he'd heard wrong.

"Mr. Lawrence, I presume?"

A small figure stood beside Lawrence, his face — or possibly her face as it was impossible to tell the sex of the person — hidden behind a shroud that covered all but the eyes.

It clearly was not Landt.

Which meant it was the person Lawrence had been waiting for.

"I have a message from Miss Diana."

The messenger's pale green eyes had a tranquillity completely unlike the swirling commotion that surrounded them.

There was a mysterious aura about the messenger; Lawrence couldn't help but feel this person was truly a messenger from the gods.

And if so — perhaps a miracle was about to happen.

"She wishes to tell you that the negotiations have failed."

A moment passed.

"What?"

"The other party is unwilling to sell. Miss Diana apologizes for being unable to live up to your expectations," said the messenger in a clear voice, as if announcing a death.

Was this — was this how it would be, then? Lawrence wondered.

True despair did not come from hopelessness.

No, when his last tiny speck of hope was crushed at the last moment — *that* was despair.

Lawrence could not reply.

The messenger seemed to understand this and turned around silently.

Somehow the messenger's form receding into the crowd became conflated in Lawrence's mind with the memory of Holo, as she'd walked away from him in the tunnels under Pazzio.

Lawrence felt like an ancient knight in rusted armor as he looked up at the price board again.

The purchase line had returned to normal, and the price continued to climb.

One could ride the changes of the market, but only the gods could control them.

Lawrence remembered the words of a famous merchant.

With just a bit more luck — just a bit more — a merchant can be a god.

Having exchanged some amount of his pyrite for coin, Amati strolled away from the stall and returned to the outer ring.

Lawrence expected the young merchant to flash him a cocky, triumphant grin, but Amati did not so much as glance at Lawrence.

There must be someone else commanding his attention.

Holo had returned to Amati's side.

"Mr. Lawrence…?"

It was Landt that now spoke to Lawrence; Holo was speaking to Amati and looked nowhere else.

"Oh, er, sorry… You've… you've done a lot of running around for me. Thanks."

"Oh no, not at all."

"Could you give Mark a message for me? Tell him my plan has failed," said Lawrence, surprised at how easy it was to say.

Yet despite the "failure," from the standpoint of a merchant it was a very nice outcome.

Lawrence still had some pyrite on hand. All he needed to do was buy a bit more to have what he needed to hand over to Amati in the evening and then subtract the cost of that from the money he'd made selling the previous lot of pyrite — the amount left over would probably be positive.

On top of that, he would be receiving one thousand silver coins from Amati, which could not be called anything less than a huge windfall.

Such profit would have been enough to make any merchant happy, but Lawrence felt only a vast emptiness.

Landt was momentarily at a loss as he looked about, but just as Lawrence was about to hand over his compensation, the boy's eyes filled with a steely resolve.

"Mr. Lawrence."

Landt's expression was enough to stop Lawrence's hand, which held a few silver coins.

"Are — are you giving up?"

Lawrence remembered his days as an apprentice — any time he wanted to make a comment, he had to be ready for a beating.

Landt was likewise prepared to be struck. His left eye twitched as if he expected a fist to come at him at any moment.

"My master always tells me that merchants never give up."

Lawrence pulled his hand away, and Landt's shoulder twitched in response.

But the boy did not look away.

He was entirely serious.

"My master always says that it's not — it's not those who pray that the god of wealth watches over. It's the stubborn ones who never give in that he blesses."

Lawrence did not disagree.

But what he was after was not wealth.

"Mr. Lawrence." Landt's gaze pierced him.

Lawrence glanced over at Holo for a moment before looking back to Landt.

"I . . ." began Landt. "I liked H-Holo from the first time I saw her. But my master told me —," said the faithful apprentice. He wordlessly completed every task given to him, yet now Landt was every inch a young boy. "He said that if I said that in front of you, I'd get a sound beating."

Landt was on the verge of tears as Lawrence raised his hand up high.

"—!" Landt gasped and flinched.

But with his fist, Lawrence only tapped the boy lightly on his cheek, smiling. "Yes, I suppose I *should* give you a beating. A sound one, too," he said with a chuckle — though he wanted to cry.

Landt seemed roughly ten years younger than Lawrence.

Yet with things the way they were, he felt no different than the boy.

Damn, he cursed himself.

It seemed that before Holo, any man would turn into a runny-nosed lad.

Lawrence shook his head.

The stubborn ones who never give in, eh?

It was a laughable phrase, and he sighed at its seductive charm, looking up at the sky.

The words of a boy ten years his junior had wiped from his mind the maelstrom of supposition and doubt.

Landt was right.

He'd gotten this far, and the profit that remained in his hands was only proof of his true loss — he could lose it without regret.

There was no reason not to think everything through one last time before taking action.

Things of value did not always come with hard effort.

Mark had only a short while ago made him realize that.

Lawrence opened the spigot on his considerable memory, pulling out the materials he needed to construct a new approach.

The pillar of his new plan was something he'd forgotten until just a moment ago.

"The ones who just can't give up — they're the same ones who just can't stop themselves from being so optimistic you wouldn't believe it," said Lawrence.

Landt's happy expression was even more appealing than the boy's normal, overachieving nature usually tended to be.

There was little doubt that Mark treasured the lad as he would his own child.

"A merchant makes plans, predicts the outcome, and always holds the results up to the light of reality. Understand?"

Landt nodded politely at what appeared to be an unconnected statement.

"If selling one item causes something to change *thus*, another item will cause it to change *so*. Such hypotheses are also important, you see."

Landt nodded again. Lawrence knelt down so he was close to the boy's face and spoke.

"But if I'm honest, these hypotheses can be anything you might like them to be. If you make too many, you'll become lost, seeing danger and risk in every deal you do. To avoid that, you need some kind of guidepost — something to believe. It's the one thing every merchant needs."

The young Landt looked something like a real merchant as he nodded. "I see," he said.

"If you can believe in that guidepost, then no matter how absurd the idea it leads you to…"

Lawrence looked up, closing his eyes.

"…You can trust it."

Even so, a voice in Lawrence's head told him it was impossible.

And yet when he looked at Holo, he was almost convinced.

There was a chance — a small chance — that Holo's choice of dress said something.

Despite the idea's outlandishness, if he was to put it to the test, it might well prove to be true.

But this idea required that one condition had to be met.

It was what Lawrence had forgotten earlier — namely, the possibility that Holo had in fact not abandoned him.

Considering this now was just the kind of thing a stubbornly optimistic merchant, who never gave up, would do.

At this stage of the game, it seemed far better to think as much than to continue trying to stop Amati — it was enough to make Lawrence think he was in some kind of fantastic dream.

He had no idea what Landt had heard from Mark that made the boy so willing to help him.

In any case, it was clear that Landt told the truth when he said he liked Holo.

It was impressive that he'd been able to admit that in front of Lawrence. Were their places reversed, Lawrence was not at all sure he would have been able to do the same.

Before a display of such courage, it was the least Lawrence could do to live up to this idea of the fearlessly optimistic merchant.

Lawrence patted Landt on the shoulder, took a deep breath, and spoke. "Once I sell my stones at the stall, start spreading the rumor I asked you to."

Landt's face lit up. He nodded his head, once again the consummate apprentice.

"Good lad."

Lawrence was about to turn around, but he stopped short.

Landt's eyes were full of questions, but Lawrence was the one who asked, "Do you believe in the gods?"

The boy was unsurprisingly dumbstruck.

Lawrence chuckled and repeated himself. "There's a good lad," he said before walking away.

He had 250 silver pieces' worth of pyrite on hand. Tallying up the purchase line markers on the board showed that there was already four hundred silver pieces' worth of orders waiting — even if Lawrence sold all the pyrite he had on hand, it would have no real effect.

But no — it *would* have an effect. If his new assumption was correct, it *had* to. He glanced back at Holo for just a moment; she was still standing by Amati.

Just one second would be enough — if Holo would just look in his direction for a moment, that would be enough.

And then —

Lawrence stood in front of the stone seller's stall. The influx of orders had slowed; the shopkeeper, having finally regained a measure of calm, looked at Lawrence with a face that said, "Yes?" He then smiled, an expression that seemed to add, "You're making out pretty well today."

Despite no words being exchanged, Lawrence nodded. He was about to make a lot more.

He thrust the bag of pyrite he'd received from Landt toward the stone seller and spoke. "I'm selling."

The shopkeeper received a cut from each transaction, so he smiled heartily and nodded, but then he looked strangely stunned.

Lawrence closed his eyes and smiled.

He had been right.

"Master, I too shall sell."

The voice actually made Lawrence nostalgic.

With a loud thud, a bag of pyrite at least twice the size of Lawrence's was slammed down on the counter.

Lawrence glanced sideways, and there was Holo, looking ready to bite his head off.

"You fool," she said.

Lawrence's only response to her accusation was a smile and a heartfelt "Sorry."

The shopkeeper stood there, amazed for a while, and then he quickly ordered his apprentices to remove all the purchase line placards from the price board.

The two bags together came to at least 650 silver pieces' worth of pyrite.

The amount Holo had was appraised before the day's bump in price, so it was probably worth even more than that. The mysterious party that had bought pyrite from Diana was, of course, Holo.

Put simply, nearly a thousand silver pieces' worth of pyrite had been sold all at once.

There was no room for demand to push the price up in the face of that.

Lawrence plucked at one of the white feathers affixed to Holo's robe. "She's quite the grown-up beauty, unlike a certain someone I could name," he said.

Holo jabbed Lawrence's side with her fist.

But then her hand remained there.

That was enough, Lawrence thought.

Though behind them a crazed mob pushed and shoved, Lawrence would not take his hand from hers.

He did want to show off to Amati, though.

Lawrence smirked at himself for being so childish.

EPILOGUE

The price crashed in an instant.

There were a few purchases that came in after all the existing purchase orders were filled, but the sale of close to one thousand silver pieces' worth of pyrite tipped the market in favor of selling, and the price soon dived.

The ones who were least fortunate—who held that old maid card in the end—were those who'd been waiting just a bit longer to sell their stock at the highest-possible price.

Even the sharp-eyed merchants who noticed Lawrence and Holo's actions and sold as quickly as they could had taken losses.

Amati's fate went without saying—he had been unable to sell off the margin contract.

Just a moment ago, Amati had been witness to Holo dashing forward with a large bag and had reached out to stop her—and there he stood in the same pose, frozen in shock.

No doubt Holo's betrayal came as a far worse shock than the margin certificate he held now turning worthless.

On that point, Lawrence had sympathy for him. Holo clearly had no intention of ever staying with him and had, in fact, separated from him in a particularly cruel way.

Evidently Amati had said something to Holo that she simply could not abide.

Lawrence didn't dare ask Holo what it was for fear of her response, but he still wanted to know, if only so he wouldn't make the same mistake himself.

"So, this contract is over, then?" Holo asked, not even bothering to look up as she groomed her tail. Lawrence had just returned from finishing the contract with Amati and thanking Mark for his trouble.

There was still an edge to Holo's voice and not just because the two had only just finished a battle of wills.

Lawrence, of course, knew the reason.

He set his things down, took a chair, and replied. "It's over, all right. As cleanly as we could ever hope."

It was not a joke.

He had indeed just finalized the contract with Amati, who looked like his spirit had left his body.

In the end, Amati hadn't actually lost money. Against the margin loss he'd taken because of Lawrence, Amati had made a bit more on intermediary sales of pyrite.

Yet Lawrence understood Amati's despair all too well — up until not long ago, he too had felt every bit as low.

In the end, Amati had been unable to meet the conditions of the contract that would've allowed him to propose marriage to Holo, and as for the margin sale of pyrite, that was completed when Lawrence handed over the bag, which was by that time essentially worthless.

He'd been worried about the possibility of Amati losing his temper, so Lawrence had asked the chief of the guild house to act as mediator. "This is your punishment for trying to take another man's woman," the guild master had said to Amati.

Whether or not Holo was in fact "Lawrence's woman," at least the proud Amati had learned a lesson.

As Lawrence briefly explained all this, Holo, who was sitting on the bed, stopped grooming her tail and gave Lawrence an appraising look.

"Surely you do not think that this is all over and done with."

She seemed to be trying to decide just how harsh his punishment should be.

Lawrence understood the mistake he had made.

He stood and raised both hands in a gesture of contrition. "I'm sorry."

Holo was unmoved. "Do you truly know where you went wrong?"

It was a pathetic way for a grown man to be scolded, but Lawrence had no choice but to endure it.

"I know."

Holo's wolf ears pricked up.

"At least... I think I know."

Holo exhaled through her nose and folded her arms in expectant displeasure.

A mere "I'm sorry" was not going to suffice.

Lawrence screwed up his courage and apologized as best he knew how.

"When I started doing things on my own after the contract with Amati, I was being utterly self-centered."

Despite the all-consuming panic he'd felt, not only had all his frantic efforts to stop Amati come to nothing, he had been — just as he said — completely self-centered.

"The point is... my biggest mistake was not trusting you."

Holo looked away, turning only a single ear toward Lawrence.

"I shall hear you out," she seemed to be saying.

Her unpleasant attitude was of course frustrating, but Lawrence had to admit he didn't have a foot to stand on.

He looked up at the ceiling before he continued.

"The feathers you attached to your hood — those were to let me know you'd bought pyrite from Diana."

Holo nodded, irritated.

"Yet when Amati sold his pyrite at the stall, trying to bluff me, I thought it was a trap you'd set for me."

"Wha —," Holo said in a small voice; Lawrence hastily shut his mouth.

He realized he'd said something he shouldn't have said, but it was too late. Holo uncrossed her legs and hung one off the edge of the bed. "What exactly do you mean by that?" she asked.

Holo's chestnut brown eyes shone dully.

"I thought it was a ruse to fool me into acting too soon. When I saw Amati make his move, I assumed you were completely on his side — the white feathers were the furthest thing from my mind. But — the truth was just the opposite... wasn't it?"

It certainly was, Holo's eyes seemed to say.

Of course, *now* he understood her intention.

"You wanted to tell me that Amati had fully enough pyrite on hand and that I should move quickly to sell mine off. Right?"

Lawrence had not trusted Holo, but Holo had trusted Lawrence.

That was the crux of the matter.

Holo had made Amati take an action that Lawrence could make no sense of, and for his part, Lawrence had decided it was not just Amati trying to destroy his confidence, but that Holo had also turned hostile and was trying to force him into a trap.

The only part Lawrence had been correct about was in assuming that Holo knew what he planned to do.

If Lawrence had but noticed the white feathers and made eye

contact with Holo, she would have sold her pyrite with him right there on the spot.

"Honestly...," muttered Holo.

She gestured with her chin for Lawrence to continue.

"And before that, the fact that you would sign the marriage certificate with Amati, that was..."

It was humiliating, but he had to keep going.

"...It was to make it easy for me to be angry...Wasn't it?"

Holo's ears twitched, and she took a deep breath.

It seemed likely that she was becoming increasingly angrier as the memories came back to her.

She must have been waiting for Lawrence to come running up to the second floor at any moment, marriage certificate in hand.

And yet no matter how long she waited, he had not come — she might have waited until dawn.

Lawrence counted himself lucky that she hadn't torn his throat out.

"Didn't I tell you in Ruvinheigen? Don't be clever and subtle all the time — tell me what you're thinking! If we can just yell at each other, problems get solved a lot faster."

Holo scratched the base of her ears, as though she could not possibly become any angrier.

She'd purposely been unperturbed when Lawrence saw Amati walking out of the inn and even had a marriage certificate ready, all to make Lawrence angry, all to make it easier for him to speak his mind.

And Lawrence had thought she was notifying him of her intentions.

And now that he thought about it, Lawrence realized that the situation there in the inn had been a perfect one — perfect for him to pour out his heart and admit to Holo that he did not want her to accept Amati's proposal.

If he'd only said as much — it would've been enough.

"So I was wrong from the start."

Holo drew in her chin and gave Lawrence a look that went past displeasure right on into resentment.

That was how far wrong he'd gone.

"When…when you lost control because of the business of Yoitsu…that last apology you gave me, that was —"

…*I am sorry*, she had said that night, her voice hoarse.

"— That was because you'd come to your senses…wasn't it?"

Holo glared at Lawrence. She glared, and her fangs showed.

After her onslaught of verbal abuse, filled with ill intent and distortions, Holo had realized how awful she was being.

Yet she had not continued to be stubborn.

She had apologized immediately with all sincerity.

But Lawrence had only made things worse by taking her apology as the final word that sealed away her heart.

He had been reaching out to her but stopped short.

If he'd managed to say something then, Lawrence thought, he might have been able to salvage the situation.

Holo must have been stunned.

She had truly apologized for the terrible things she said after losing her temper, but instead of accepting the apology, Lawrence had backed out of the room and run.

She was no fool; Holo must have seen that Lawrence misunderstood her.

Yet having realized this, Holo thought that chasing Lawrence down just to explain how he was mistaken would have been ridiculous.

She must have assumed he would realize his mistake much sooner.

Her eyes were now full of anger at Lawrence's failure to see this.

"You — you fool!" she shouted, standing up from the bed. "They say, 'A fool's errand is worse than sloth,' it is even so! Not only did you render useless my efforts, but you thought I was your enemy? And then for some reason, you go and pursue that contract with the boy! Do you have any notion how difficult that made things for me? We may have only met recently, you and I, but I'm of the feeling that we share an uncommon bond! Am I deluding myself? Or do you really —"

"I wish to continue traveling with you."

There were only a few steps between the desk and the bed.

Human and wolf, merchant and nonmerchant — separated by only a few steps.

If Lawrence but reached his hand out, it would soon reach her.

"My life has been naught but business from dawn to dusk, and I plan to keep it that way. Just think of me as a little slow when it comes to anything *besides* business."

Holo's expression turned sulky.

"And yet — I do wish to travel with you."

"Well... what *am* I to you?"

It was the question he'd been unable to answer.

Now, however, he was completely certain.

"It cannot be explained in words."

Holo's eyes widened, her ears pricked up, and then —

And then she laughed, so frustrated with Lawrence she was fit to cry. "What sort of dried-up old line is that?"

"Ah, but I thought dried jerky was your favorite!"

Holo chuckled, her fangs bared, her mouth very near Lawrence's hand. "I hate it!"

Lawrence felt pain shoot through his palm, but he quietly accepted it as his punishment.

"Though I do have one question for you," said Lawrence finally.

"Oh?" said Holo. She looked up after biting Lawrence's hand with considerable anger.

"How did you know there was pyrite in the alchemists' quarter — wait, no, Amati probably told you. What I want to know is, how did you get Diana to sell it to you? I just can't see it."

Holo looked out the window as if to say, "Oh, that?"

Dusk had arrived, and the second evening's festivities were about to begin.

It seemed that the same giant puppets from the first night were being used, though they were much the worse for wear. Half of the large lupine shapes had lost their heads. The participants' fatigue was obvious, even from a distance, as they tottered along. Some even fell on their bottoms — and not in jest.

Yet the column marched on, pulled forward by the sounds of flutes and drums.

Holo looked back to Lawrence; her eyes beckoned him to join her at the window.

Having no reason to refuse, he did so.

"The boy Amati told me everything he knew, so I was able to make a fair guess at what you were planning. But your plan was, well — I should compliment you."

Holo looked out on the festival as she leaned back into Lawrence.

He was unable to see her expression, but having been complimented, he felt he should accept it as gracefully as he could manage.

"Yes, so — Diana, was it? I went to see her for a different reason truthfully."

"A different reason?"

"I suppose you could call it a favor. I tracked down the location from the scent on the letter. The place stank like the worst hot springs — it was far from enjoyable."

While Lawrence was impressed at Holo's keen sense of smell, he had to admit the alchemists' quarter must have been quite an ordeal for her.

Holo sighed softly and continued, not looking at Lawrence. "So

I asked her thus. I asked her if she would not invent a story of Yoitsu still existing and if she would pass it on to you."

Lawrence cocked his head for a moment, confused.

But then he understood.

Had he heard such a tale from Diana, he would surely have found it easier to speak to Holo again.

With that as a trigger, he would've needed nothing more.

"However," continued Holo, her tone suddenly irritated. "That *girl* just had me explain all the circumstances to her only to turn me down."

"Oh...really?" Lawrence thought back on the words Diana had spoken to him as he left her house: *Good luck to you.*

Had it been sarcasm?

"It was your fault that I was refused! Consider that, why don't you!"

Lawrence was jolted from his reverie by Holo stomping on his foot—though he did not follow her meaning.

"Honestly...I suffer through the humiliation of explaining everything and am on the very cusp of success, then *you* show up and make that *girl* come up with her pointless plan."

He was stunned beyond words—Holo had been there when he'd visited Diana?

"She said it would be good to test your resolve—the *gall*, acting as if she knows me!"

Lawrence now understood whence came Diana's *Good luck to you.*

But he felt like he was forgetting something important.

"I also heard that foolish question you put to her."

"Ah—!" Lawrence shouted, his voice strangled.

Holo grinned devilishly and turned around to face Lawrence. "So there are many stories of gods and humans becoming mates, eh?" Her upward-cast eyes were frightening.

She slid her slender arms around Lawrence, like a snake entrapping its prey.

"If that is how you feel, I would not mind. Though I'd ask…"

The light that fell through the window cast a red glow over Holo's features.

"…I'd ask you to be gentle with me."

She must really be a demon, Lawrence thought to himself half-seriously — but she soon dropped her act.

"Mm. I just cannot seem to rouse myself after talking to that girl," said Holo, looking tired as she gazed out the window, her arms still around Lawrence.

She seemed to be looking not at the festival, but somewhere far away.

"Did you notice that she was not human?" Holo finally said.

Lawrence couldn't even manage a "surely not."

"You saw the feathers scattered about her room, yes? Those were hers."

"…They were?"

Although now that Holo mentioned it, Lawrence recalled that something about Diana had made him think of a bird.

Holo nodded and continued, "Her true form is a bird, much larger than you. She fell in love with a traveling monk and spent many years building a church with him, but eventually he noticed that no matter how many years passed, the girl never aged — thus the monk grew suspicious. No doubt you can guess the rest."

Lawrence felt Holo's arms tighten around him.

He thought he now understood the reason why Diana collected stories and why she protected the alchemists so.

But it would be painful to say it. Surely Holo did not want to hear it, either.

Lawrence said nothing.

Instead, he simply put his arm around Holo's shoulders.

"I wish to return to my homeland. Even…even if it's no longer there."

"We will."

Outside the window, the giant human and lupine puppets collided, and a great cheer arose.

But Lawrence realized the display was not reenacting some battle.

The people controlling these battered puppets were all laughing, and each onlooker seemed to have a cup of ale in hand.

They were not hitting each other, but putting their arms about one another's shoulders.

Soon they began to sing and dance, and the giant puppets in the center of the intersection were set ablaze.

Holo giggled. "Humans are so showy."

"They surely are."

Despite their distance from the intersection, Lawrence could feel the heat of the flames on his cheeks.

The ring of revelers that surrounded the fire gave a great cheer, and the bonfire itself seemed intense enough to overpower the pale moon.

Once again in the town of Kumersun, various gods and humans from near and far had come together to drink and celebrate after putting an end to their quarreling.

The conflicts were finally over.

"Shall we go?" asked Holo.

"I suppose we shall?"

But Holo did not immediately move. She looked up at the puzzled Lawrence. "For my part, I would not mind you being as passionate as those flames."

The flaming puppets had begun to collapse into a single pile.

Lawrence laughed. "I suppose if I were drunk enough."

Holo laughed, her sharp fangs flashing. Her tail wagged as she

spoke, delighted. "If you become drunk, who's to watch over me? Fool!"

Lawrence took the laughing Holo's hand and led her out of the room.

The Kumersun night had once again been set ablaze with festivities.

Some time thereafter, it was spoken of in rumors that a true goddess had walked amid the crowds.

AFTERWORD

It has been a while! I'm Isuna Hasekura, and this is the third volume, which makes it the third story in the series.

This time I feel like I was able to write without forgetting the personalities of the characters. Instead of that, I've managed to forget the deadline for this afterword, and just a moment ago, I got a phone call from my editor, whose unfriendly smile I felt I could hear over the phone.

I'm starting to wonder if I'm not just going to be forgotten by the readers.

Well then, volume 3 means there are three books, of which this is the third novel. Around this time last year, I'd passed the first-round selection for the Dengeki Novel Prize and was camped out next to the phone, waiting for the results of the second-round selection. Back then, writing even one volume was a major effort — I'd write, then throw it away, write again, then throw it away again.

So since the end of last year, I've been writing at a nigh-heroic pace, and even in that year, I feel like maybe I've grown up just a bit.

My latest hobby is surfing real estate sites. And not normal ones. I'm talking about the big time — hundred-million-yen condos and mansions.

I like the view from high places, so I was thinking I'd like to live someday in a high-rise condo with a view of the city lights at night. I've been looking at model homes along those lines, and they're crazy. Everything's just done up in this unimaginably overwhelming fashion, and before I knew it, I was sucked in.

The prices had so many zeros I was rubbing my eyes just to make sure my vision still worked right, and when I saw the mere two-hundred-yen neighborhood association fee, I was genuinely relieved. Somehow I felt like I could work hard and keep on living. When I realized that using the parking lot and wine cellar (it had a wine cellar, guys!) of one of these mansions would cost more than the rent of my entire apartment, well, I guess I'm just a commoner at heart. I hope you'll all bear with me.

And now, my thanks.

To illustrator Jyuu Ayakura-sensei, thank you for making time in the midst of your busy schedule to draw such wonderful pictures. They make me want to have my writing be worthy of them every day.

And to my editor, Koetsu-sama. For your patient grammatical guidance, I thank you. As basic corrections to my Japanese become less and less frequent, I will devote myself more thoroughly to everything that comes after those corrections.

Finally to all of my readers, thank you for taking this book into your hands.

Let us meet again in the next volume.

Isuna Hasekura

Isuna Hasekura

Born December 27, 1982. Winner of the twelfth Dengeki Novel Prize Silver Medal. Studying physics at college, he's a romantic who up until recently believed that the sky was blue because it was reflecting the color of the ocean. He remains opposed to negative ions and oxygenated water.

Works from Dengeki Bunko:

Spice and Wolf
Spice and Wolf, Volume 2
Spice and Wolf, Volume 3

Illustrator: Jyuu Ayakura

Born 1981. Birthplace: Kyoto. Blood Type: AB. Currently living a free, spartan life in Tokyo, he has been thus far unsuccessful in putting his temple-hiking plans into action.

THE JOURNEY CONTINUES IN THE MANGA
ADAPTATION OF THE HIT NOVEL SERIES

SPICE & WOLF

MATURE
M
Yen
Press